# NEMESIS III

*Summit Of The Murder Game*

# NEMESIS III

*Summit Of The Murder Game*

By

Tehuti Atum-Ra

# NEMESIS III
## SUMMIT OF THE MURDER GAME

This is a work of fiction. The author have invented the characters. Any resemblance to actual persons living, deceased, or similarities to actual events, and places is purely coincidental and are intended to give the novel a sense of reality.

Self-published with help from
Midnight Express Books
POBox 69
Berryville, AR 72616
http://www.MidnightExpressBooks.com
Email: MEBooks1@yahoo.com

# NEMESIS III

*Summit Of The Murder Game*

By

Tehuti Atum-Ra

# PROLOGUE

August 1972

New Orleans, Louisiana

Immediately after the judge entered the courtroom by way of his chambers, the bailiff shouted, "All rise!" The entire courtroom immediately stood. Including the defendant, Leonard 'Jaedm' Denson, and his well respected Louisiana Attorney, Larry Calmstock.

Once the judge took his seat behind the bench, everyone was ordered to be seated. There was complete silence in the courtroom as everyone awaited the jury. "Bailiff," the judge immediately spoke up. "You may bring in the jury." As the bailiff hurried to a side door in back of the courtroom, all heads turned in his direction. As the twelve jurors slowly entered the courtroom, it was a tense moment. The judge, court-officers and every spectator from both sides of the courtroom tried to read the juror's expression as they slowly took their respective seats behind the jury-box.

The defendant, however, appeared at eased. For him, it was an easy read as he sat comfortably in his chair, patiently awaiting his fate.

"Have the jury reached a verdict?" asked the judge.

The jury foreman, a young chubby black man sporting a huge afro that had been hot-combed to appear larger than its actual size, stood. Without displaying any emotion, Jaedm gazed at him with boredom and nothing more. "Yes sir, your honor. We have," said the foreman before handing the bailiff a note on a small piece of paper. The Bailiff quickly rushed over to the bench and handed the note to the judge.

After the judge unfolded the small piece of paper and looked at it. He then glanced at the defendant, Jaedm. Who, neither he nor his attorney displayed the least bit of concern. Agitated by the defendants arrogance, the judge immediately turned to the jury and asked, "In the case of State Vs. Denson, on the count of Murder in the first degree, how do you find the defendant?"

The Foremen quickly stood again and shouted, "Not guilty, your honor!"

The outrage in the court had been so disruptive, the judge began banging his gavel while shouting, "ORDER! ORDER IN THE COURT!"

"Yeah! Yeah! Not guilty, nigga! Yeah!" someone shouted from the back of the courtroom.

"ORDER! ORDER!" the judge continue to yell. Once the verbalized sentiments of spectators calmed. The judge immediately warned, "One more out-burst like that and I will clear this courtroom." He then turned towards the twelve jurors and thanked them for their services before relieving them of their duties. As the jury slowly left the courtroom. He turned to Jaedm and his lawyer, Larry Calmstock and said, "Will the defendant please rise." Both Jaedm and his lawyer immediately stood. "Mr. Denson," he began, "having been found not guilty by a jury of your peers, it is here by ordered by the state of Louisiana that you are free to go. Case dismissed!"

After the judge slowly rose from behind the bench and disappeared into his chambers. Jaedm's lawyer smiled and patted him on the back. The twenty-four year old killer glanced over at the attractive, thirty-two year old female District Attorney and winked. She, along with those who supported the prosecution, rolled their eyes with contempt while whispering their outrage amongst themselves. A few supporters of Jaedm rushed over to congratulate him on his victory.

"Come on, let me give you a ride home," his lawyer said while gesturing with his hand for Jaedm to lead the way.

Mona Leigh, and her second chair stared at the young hoodlum and his expensive mouth-piece as both men confidently walked out of the courtroom. She knew she had a weak case against Jaedm, but she thought it was a shot worth taking. Her only regrets was wasting tax payer's money in her quest to put a senseless killer away for life. Still, she did manage to rest comfortably in the knowledge knowing, because Leonard 'Jaedm' Denson was a murdering hoodlum. It was just a matter of time before he slipped up again. And this time, she silently swore, I'll be well prepared to bury him.

Outside the courthouse, the press were everywhere. Larry Calmstock was a senior partner at a successful, well respected, high-powered Louisiana law firm. Who, along with his colleagues, wore nothing less than one-thousand dollar suits. As soon as word got out that his firm had been representing a street thug in a black on black murder trial. They wanted to know why? No one knew Larry Calmstock and his firm had been secretly retained to represent the young hoodlum. And he nor his firm had no intentions of divulging that information.

Immediately after spotting Calmstock coming out of the courthouse with his client. Someone from the press shouted, "There they are!" All eyes Simultaneously zeroed in on the well dressed lawyer and his client. But by the time they were able to reach them, both men had pulled off in a white Mercedes that had been waiting out front.

While the driver cruised down the street, Jaedm finally turned to his lawyer and thanked him for coming to his aid. "I owe you one, man. If that bitch woulda' got that conviction? I woulda' been finished, you dig where um' comin' from? Remind me to get you a nice gold watch."

Without looking at Jaedm, Calmstock casually replied, "My fee for representing you Mr. Denson, has already been paid by someone who wish to remain anonymous."

"It wouldn't happen to be a woman, would it?" Jaedm already knew his answer.

"That information I cannot provide. Your benefactor was adamant about the firm maintaining anonymity." He finally looked at Jaedm and said, "I will say this, they were more than generous retaining my firm to get you off. Now that the job has been completed. Our business is concluded. But, if I may offer you a small piece of advice. I suggest you leave New Orleans."

Jaedm looked at him strangely, "Now why would I want to do something like that?" he replied.

"Listen to me and listen closely, Mr. Denson. The District Attorney will be out for blood. Mona Leigh is a very powerful young woman who does not like to lose. Which is why she rarely does."

Jaedm slowly looked at him and asked, "Do I look like a man who give a fuck about a bitch like your Mona Lisa. Man, fuck that bitch."

Calmstock looked away and slowly shook his head from side to side. It was apparent he had not only wasted his breath, but also the hard work and time he had put into Jaedm's case in getting him off. "How do you feel?" he changed the subject.

Jaedm smiled. "Like killin' somebody else," he said while gazing that the attorney.

"I didn't hear that," said Calmstock while turning his back on Jaedm to look out the window. "You were lucky today, Mr. Denson," he continued while turning to look at Jaedm again. "Take my advice and leave, at least for a while. After things cool down a bit, come back."

"I don't think so," Jaedm said defiantly.

"As your lawyer, I am only looking out for your best interest." As the lawyer continued, Jaedm thought about all the people he was going to murder. All the people who had crossed him in one way, or another. They thought he was finished but he always managed to pop up when they lease expected.

"You really think I should leave?"

"Just for a few years, maybe longer. By then, the District Attorney would have focused on someone else and forgotten all about you."

"The D.A., huh?" he thought aloud. He was beginning to give the idea some thought, but his mind kept coming up with excuses not to. "All my enemies are here. If I leave umma' have to make some new ones," he laughed aloud.

"That's funny," said the lawyer. "Most people try to avoid trouble?"

As much as Jaedm did not want to admit it, the lawyer was right. Everyone in law-enforcement wanted a piece of him. Deep down, he knew it was just be a matter of time before his past caught up with him. "Any suggestions?" he asked.

The lawyer reached into his expensive suit jacket pocket and pulled out an envelope. Jaedm immediately spotted the name, JAEDM typed in bold, upper case letters on the front of it.

"That for me?" he quickly asked the obvious while reaching for it.

"Think of it as a life changing opportunity."

"Opportunity to what? Who gave you this?" he had an idea who the envelop came from. Just as he had an idea who provided the talent for his defense. He just wasn't sure about Calmstock.

"Why don't you open it and find out?"

"Maybe later," he said while folding the envelop in half before placing it into his pocket. He smiled to himself, resting comfortably in the fact that Calmstock was as curious as he had initially suspected. Which was why he decided to read it later.

While the driver headed towards the Ninth Ward, both Jaedm and his attorney road in silence. Calmstock glanced at him briefly while wondering why Jaedm declined to open the envelope in front of him. He wanted to ask, but was afraid of offending Jaedm by prying. After working very close with Jaedm during the course of the trial. It was apparent Jaedm was a loaded gun with a hair-trigger and Calmstock couldn't wait to be rid of him.

"Tell that nigga' to pull over." Jaedm ordered.

"Are you sure, Mr. Denson?" asked Calmstock. Jaedm stared coldly at the attorney as if he had just been insulted. If it was one thing he couldn't stand, that would be repeating himself. Once Calmstock saw the look in Jaedm's eyes he quickly yelled to his driver, "Driver, pull over."

The moment the driver pulled over to the curb, Jaedm jumped out and began hastily walking up the street. He briefly glanced at the white Mercedes as it drove pass and was happy to be out of the company of what he considered, a pompous piece of shit.

Jaedm didn't get less than two blocks before he spotted his young partner, Mazeroti. The eighteen year old Mazeroti had just walked up on a group of young hustlers slinging nickel and dime bags of 'skag' on the block. It was the way Mazeroti had approached the group that gave away his intentions. Afraid Mazeroti would be forced into a situation he could not get out without the blaze of his gun. Jaedm quickened his pace, but it was too late. Mazeroti threw a left hook to one of the kid's jaw, sending him stumbling backwards to the concrete pavement. As the youth laid on the ground dazed, Mazeroti reached for the pistol tucked in his waistband. But before he had a chance to pull out. The kid he had just assaulted three buddies quickly interrupted his flow. Mazeroti looked around and saw three angry faces armed with 'Saturday Night Specials' aimed directly at him. But that didn't stop Mazeroti from pulling out on the kid he was beefing with. "You out gunned, Maz'. Let it go," said the kid while managing to finally climb to his feet.

"Yeah, but you'll be the first to get it in the face." Mazeroti calmly said while boldly advanced towards the kid with his gun raised high and tilted to the side. "Didn't I tell you not to fuck with me, nigga!" he warned.

"Hold up, Cuz!" shouted the youth. "You beefin' with the wrong cat. Your beef is with that fake ass pimp, Mink! Not me."

"Who?"

"That nigga' Mink, man."

Mazeroti cut an eye at the kid's three young buddies and shouted, "You three stiff-ass-muthafuckaz gonna' shoot, SHOOT!" he stared at the three gun-man like a madman. He knew none of them didn't really have the heart to actually pull the trigger. They were hustlers, not killers. He, on the other hand was a stone cold killer and they all knew it. They just never counted on him having a death wish. "SHOOT, MUTHAFUCKA'! SHOOT!," he roared like a ferocious beast foaming from the mouth. All four men looked at one another "No balls, lil' niggaz'? I can dig it. Let Maz' show you how real niggaz' roll." Just as he cocked the hammer back, the kid's three friends turned and ran down the street. Mazeroti laughed before turning to the kid he had previously assaulted.

"Hold up, Maz'! I..."

"MAZ!" Jaedm appeared out of nowhere breathing hard as if he had been running. Without turning his head, Mazeroti briefly glanced to his right and saw his idol, Jaedm. "Let it go, Lil' bruh'. We got real work to put in," Jaedm reminded while heading to Mazeroti's car. Mazeroti grinned coldly at the young hustler, un-cocked the hammer to his weapon and lowered it. Then, as if nothing had ever happened, turn and walked off to his car where Jaedm waited in the back seat.

Before getting into his car. He tucked the chrome plated .38 in the waist of his pant. Then pulled his shirt over the front of his trousers to conceal it. Without so much as a glance back at the kid, he got in and backed out of his parking space.

As he slowly pulled off. The young hustler, whom everyone referred to as Red, shouted with his gun aimed at the car as it drove pass. "Yeah nigga'! You stole me, right!"

Jaedm, who sat in the back seat of the black 1968 Lincoln, opened the envelope his lawyer had previously given him. After reading the note, he placed it back into the envelop, ripped it into several tiny pieces before opening the window to toss it out. The kid's voice could still be heard as Mazeroti slowly cruised down the street. Jaedm turned in his seat to glance at the kid who could still be heard yelling at the car while waving his gun in the air. "Who's your lil' friend?" Jaedm asked.

"Some lil' punk-ass pusher name, Red. He likes to get young girls strung-out so he can control 'em. He ain't 'bout nothin'," said Mazeroti while briefly glancing at Jaedm in the rear-view before changing the subject. "Nice to have you back, man. Shit was real boring with you lock-down. Jokers thought you were done."

"And you, Maz'? What did you think?"

Surprised Jaedm would even ask such a question, Mazeroti looked at his mentor in the rear-view again and said, "You already know, Big Bruh. You already know."

"Yeah. I heard about you. You did me a real solid."

"Shit! If it came down to it. I'd ran up in that courtroom with guns blazing, you dig?"

"Solid on that, man."

"You'd done the same for me."

"Let's hope it never come to that."

"And if it do?" Mazeroti playfully asked.

Jaedm smiled a crooked smile and shouted, "JAEDM-UP, MUTHAFUCKAZ'!" Mazeroti laughed before proceeded to fill Jaedm in on how he had to murdered the three state's witnesses and threaten two of the jurors families to find him not guilty. Jaedm had to admit, he was impressed. If there was one thing Mazeroti was lacking, heart was not it. The young hoodlum was fearless. But unlike Jaedm, who trained Mazeroti to be a killer. He did not lack a conscience and Jaedm didn't mind or try to change the eighteen year old bull who he regarded as his little brother. The fact that he was fearless was good enough.

"Where you wanna' go, Jaedm?"

First stop, the Quarters."

They parked on Royal Street, about eight blocks from New Orleans Historic Voodoo Museum. "Wait here," Jaedm ordered as he exit the car and began walking down the street. Mazeroti watched as Jaedm stopped at a single-story, Creole cottage style house that was probably built during the eighteen hundreds. While Jaedm waited for someone to answer the door, Mazeroti carefully looked around. The last thing he wanted was for one of Jaedm's enemies to pop up out of nowhere. When someone finally answered the door, Jaedm walked into the house.

Mazeroti had dropped Jaedm off at the house more times than he could count, but never knew who occupied the residence. Because Jaedm never talked about it, Mazeroti never asked. His encounters at the house was his own business. The way Mazeroti saw it, if Jaedm wanted him to know he would have told him a long time ago.

While sitting behind the wheel awaiting Jaedm's return. Mazeroti couldn't shake feeling someone was behind him. Without thinking twice, he quickly pulled out his weapon, released the safety and cocked the hammer while glancing in his side-view mirror. No one was there. When he glanced in the rear-view and saw a beautiful, young, dark-skinned woman sitting in the back seat staring back at him, his heart skipped a beat.

Without thinking twice, he tried to twisted in his seat with his gun drawn ready to fire on the uninvited, but found himself unable to move or speak. Shocked by the beautiful woman's presence his first thoughts were how she manage to get into his car without him noticing? The woman had a flawless, blue-black completion that appeared to have a natural glow. Her three inch crop was jet- black and styled in a natural. Her lips were full, perfectly shaped and cherry-red in color.

As he stared at her in the rear-view, her dark penetrating gaze  stared back,  terrifying  him. "Am I to understand you are not  a  believer?" she  spoke  with a heavy accent he could not identify.  He didn't know how, but he was sure she knew his every thought.  Including  his  main concern at the moment which had been for Jaedm's safety. How she managed to sneak into his car without  him knowing was no longer important. "Yah' don't have to worry 'bout yah' friend, seen. He be sittin' in me front-room, sip'pin on a hot cup of green-tea. Before yah' know it, he be get'tin back to yah', and  dah' both of yah' be get'tin back' to yah business with no  conscious knowledge of me, or what I have to say. So listen,  me-youth.  and  listen closely. Today be dah' day yah' friend becomes a fa'dah."

The sound of the car door opening, woke Mazeroti. "Damn, lil' bruh', you must be tired?" Jaedm pointed out while getting into the back seat. "That ain't like you," he continued. "Dozing off like that. You 'pose to be on point, you dig?"

"Um' hip." Mazeroti  agreed. Still a little groggy, he start  the  car and  noticed his gun cocked in his hand. "Damn! I must be trippin'."

"Why? What's happen?"

"Ain't nothin'," Mazeroti assured while safely securing his weapon before  starting  the  car. "How  long  you  been  gone?" he   curiously asked,  hoping  it  would give him an idea how long he had been asleep.

"Shit, no more than three to five minute. That's why I said you must be tired. I ain't been gone that long."

"Where to now?" he asked without giving his unexplained fatigue any more thought.

"Keep driving. Nigga' been locked down nine months. Um' in desperate need to have my pipe cleaned, you dig." It's a motel a few blocks up. I know this head-hunter who can polish a knob so good, shit makes your toes curl, you dig what um' sayin'?"

"I can dig it." Mazeroti drove a few blocks up the street until he spotted a sleazy motel. He was hoping that was by no means the motel Jaedm was talking about.

"That's it right there."

"This dump? I wouldn't touch a bitch who stayed here," Mazeroti said as he pulled onto the trashy lot.

"I didn't say she lived here. I said she hangs out around here," Jaedm reminded.

Mazeroti parked, cut the engine and looked around. It was early noon, hardly any activity going on. "Now what?"

Jaedm scanned the area. There were a few people hanging around. None of which were the woman he was looking for. "I don't see her. It is kinda' early, you know what 'um sayin'." He was about to instruct Mazeroti to leave until he spotted two women coming out of one of the rooms. "Damn! Who the fuck is that?" he immediately asked before adding, "She can't be no hooker?"

"Who? Where?

"Right there. Standing next to that thick, pale bitch in the purple hot-pant."

It did not take long for Mazeroti to zero in on the young, thick, light-skinned female wearing the purple hot-pant that was so tight, her firm yellow ass-cheeks were clearly exposed. He then noticed a tall white girl standing next to her. "You talkin' 'bout that skinny-ass white bitch in the blue-jean?" he asked.

"Hell yeah. Damn she's a fox. Check her out. She fine, right?"'

"Bitch look like a junky, Jaedm. You buggin'. Besides, they too young, man. And damn sure ain't got no business 'round here, you know what um' sayin'?"

"Definitely out of place," Jaedm muttered while staring at the skinny white girl. She was the most beautiful female he had ever seen and was praying she was of age.

As he proceeded to get out of the car, Mazeroti abruptly stopped him. "Hold up, player. They just kids, man?"

"Don't worry, Maz'. Before I put my rap down, I wanna' see some I.D., you dig."

"Play on, player," Mazeroti teased while Jaedm got out of the car.

"You think I ain't," Jaedm replied before closing the car door and heading towards the two females.

Jaedm, pronounced Jay'dim, was a twenty-four year old paid killer who worked for no one in particular. Born in the French Quarter of New Orleans, he was raised in a boarding house on Toulouse Street by an abusive drunk of a father who took pleasure in physically abusing his only son.

Jaedm never knew his mother. Who, according to his father, died from an over-dose two years after he was born. Nine years later, Jaedm have had enough of the unprovoked beating from the heavy hand of his father's belt.

With just the clothes on his back, he immediately left the French Quarter shortly after murdering his father with a .22 he stole from a neighbor a few days before. It was 1959 and Jaedm was just eleven at the time. With no family or friends to take him in, he found himself roaming the mean streets of the ninth-ward section of New Orleans. That same night, a dynamic, eighteen year old female gangster named, Patti Johnson found him standing in the rain.

By the time Jaedm was sixteen, he had made a name for himself in the murder-game while his mentor, boss, and friend became a legion.

Mazeroti watched as Jaedm approached the two young girls. He didn't have the heart to tell Jaedm, along with a number of other young hoods around the way, he already knew one of the females. He personally have had his eye on the light-skinned 'chick' for some time now. And like most of the others young bulls in the 'hood, he patiently waited for the thick red-bone whom the streets called, Frenchie to come of age before making his move. Which was why he had been so up-set with the young hustler, Red earlier. He warned Red on a number of occasions to stay away from her. But like the others, Red was determined to have her. Even if it meant putting shit in the game by trying to get her stung-out. Mazeroti knew what the young pusher was up to. What he didn't know was, someone had already succeeded.

As Jaedm talked to the two young females. Mazeroti suddenly came down with a case of, déjà-vu. There was something very familiar about the present moment. He just couldn't connect the dots.

Moments later Jaedm returned to the car feeling good about himself. He had both of the female's name, and a date set up for the night. "She's French-Creole, you dig. You can have the other one."

"Damn, Jaedm. You really like that skinny-ass-bitch? You trippin." said Mazeroti.

"She turn me on, man. What can I say." said Jaedm while watching the two young girls who casually chatted and giggled while leaving the area. Every now and then they would glance back at Jaedm, then giggle.

"No offense, big bruh', but that bitch ain't got no ass." Mazeroti was quick to point out.

"Damn sure don't," Jaedm agree while staring at the young, thin, white girl. "but she got some pretty-ass eyes. You shoulda' seen 'em, Maz'. Fuck the ass. The bitch face turn me on."

Mazeroti stared at the white female for a moment. "That broad look strung-out, man. You sure she ain't no junkie? Bitch probably fuckin' out of both drawls."

"Naw' man," Jaedm quickly jumped in to defend his young, skinny, prize. "She ain't like that. Neither one of 'em is."

Mazeroti looked at Jaedm. He wanted to ask, how you know? but knew Jaedm hated being questioned. So he played along by changing the subject. "So what's her name?"

"She said her friends call her, Cat. When you see those eyes? You'll see why she got the handle. Dig this, her friend there? The one I set you up with is, Frenchie. I like my bitches with sexy-ass names, you dig?"

"I can dig it."

"Said they lived here all their lives. I can believe that. They just ain't the kind of girls we use to, you know."

"I hear you." Mazeroti stared at the woman for a moment. "Cat and Frenchie, huh...." he thought aloud before looking at Jaedm asking, "You ready to roll?"

"Yeah. Let's go kill somebody. Fuck it!" Both men laughed as Mazeroti pulled out of the lot.

# CHAPTER 1

The inconspicuous stranger watched as TooSweet made her way up the street in the direction of a white '92 Accord, He continued to watch until he suddenly noticed her slowing down to look over her shoulder at the two sedans that had not pulled off yet. He took his eyes off of her long enough to retrieve a Russian assault rifle from under a blanket in the back seat of his car. Something's wrong? he silently thought while cocking the riffle.

Once TooSweet realized the men in the two sedans were still watching, a bad feeling came over her. As she approached the Honda, she saw a man sitting behind the wheel. Because the man had his back to her, she was unable to see his face. Realizing it could be a set-up, her first thoughts were to run, but her instincts told her to play it out. "After all," she reasoned, "if it was a sit-up, why the charade? If they wanted me dead, they had plenty of time and opportunity in the car?" Unarmed, she walked up to the window on the driver's side of the Honda and knocked on the glass with her index knuckle, then waited. The man sitting behind the wheel immediately turned to face her. As soon as she saw his face, she smiled and rushed around to the passenger side of the car and got in.

"Sorry I'm late, Ms. Strong." said the man while gathering up some papers he had scattered on the front seat.

"Actually," she began "Your timing couldn't have been better. What the hell is going on?"

With a slight hesitancy, he answered her question with a question. "You tell me? My wife and I were enjoying dinner with the United States District Attorney and his wife. The next thing I know, I'm on the phone with T. Sharp," he lied.

"Tyrone?"

"Said he wanted me to arrange a trade-off. You for a disk that contained some very damaging information against some very important people."

"I know about the disk, but how the hell did you know I was about to be arrested? How did you even know where to find me?" None of it made sense to TooSweet. The attorney's timing was just too perfect.

"That you'll have to ask Mr. Sharp. I just follow instructions. Now, where can I drop you?"

She looked out the back window down the street. The two Fords had left. "I left my car a few blocks down. It's right across the street from a restaurant called, MAMA'S PLACE."

As they drove, TooSweet couldn't resist asking, "Did you look at the disk?"

"I had to," he replied without taking his eyes from the road. "Couldn't very well make a fool out of myself by bothering the D.A. with something not worth his time, or mine." He looked at her briefly before continuing. "I don't think Mr. Sharp actually knew what he had."

TooSweet was insult by the implication. "We knew," she quickly replied while adding, "We also knew arresting the people on that disk should be far more important than trying to indict me for something they know I didn't do."

After parking in front of MAMA'S PLACE. He turned to her and asked, "Have you ever heard of a man by the name of, Johnathen Crain, Ms. Strong?"

She thought hard and long. The name sounded very familiar. She just couldn't remember where she had heard that name? "Maybe. Why?" she asked, more curious now than ever.

"He was the reason the D.A. took an interest in the agreement for the disk."

"I don't understand. Who is he?"

"A respectable attorney and the son of a very important man here in the city. The District Attorney's office are well familiar with a lot of the names on the disk. Most of which are suspected of a host of crimes ranging from money laundering, illegal narcotics, to murder and tax evasion. Unfortunately they can't  move on the indictments without implicating Mr. Crain?"

"I'm sorry, am I missing something?"

"Apparently  so. The Crain's name being on the disk complicate things. If he goes down. You can rest assured a lot of people will follow. A lot of good name's will be dragged through the mud. It's a shame because the D.A. has never been able to make a case against a lot of the names on the disks."

"So what now?"

"Well... let's just say there will be no federal indictments. The D.A. feels, if he indicted someone on the disk, they may implicate Mr. Crain. I guess he's not willing to take that chance. Which puts him back at square one. It could be very embarrassing for a host of important people. Including the judge who signed the federal court order for your immunity."

"So they just gonna' let it go? Like nothing never happened?" she asked.

"I wouldn't worry about it, Ms. Strong. The important thing is, you are not in jail. Which means... I've done my job," he looked at her and smiled.

"Well... I hope everything work out. And thanks again for coming to my rescue, Mr. Vincent," she said while exiting the car.

"Thank Mr. Sharp. I was just doing what I'm paid to do. Which reminds me? I was told to give you a message." He reached for the slip of paper on the dashboard and looked at it. "Here we go. C.C.P, ASAP. Does that mean anything?"

"Yes, thanks." She closed the car door and stood on the curb watching as he waved to her just before pulling off.

On her way across the street to her car, she noticed something very strange. One of the sky-blue sedans she left a few blocks up the street, was now parked about five cars behind her. She couldn't quite tell how many men sat in the car, but there were definitely more than one person. The thought had occurred that they could have been there on other business that had nothing to do with her. Intuition, however, told her different.

Without stopping, she immediately got into her car and fired up the engine. Before pulling off, she watched the car in the side view mirror and noticed two of the Federal agents getting out. When they proceeded to advance in her direction, it was time for her to leave.

Boxed in, she threw the car in drive. Then forced the steering-wheel all the way to the right and floored it. As the car pulled off without touching the car parked in front of her. She navigated the steering-wheel to the left and sped off down the street while glancing in her rear-view. Just before turning the corner, she caught a glimpse of them. They had just gotten back into their car and were now in pursuit. She had no idea why they were chasing her, but knew it couldn't have been anything good. She also knew there was no way she could out-run them in her car on a city street. Her chances of losing them would be much better on foot.

Unarmed and unprepared, she quickly parked on Amsterdam and jumped out of her car. She was about to run across the street when a black 'Cuda pulled up out of nowhere and screeched to a halt directly in front of her. "GET IN!" shouted a middle aged, dark skinned men sporting baby dreadlocks. At first, she hesitated. But when the sky-blue Ford screeched around the corner in pursuit of her, it was a 'no brainer'. As soon as she slid into the front seat of the 'Cuda, the car quickly sped off.

"Nice car," she said looking out the back window to see if the Federal agents were still pursuing. She then looked at her driver and said, "You do know the Feds are chasing me?"

"Feds," he glanced at her. "Those cats ain't no damn Feds. Try freelancers."

"Freelancers? I hope you don't mean Murder for hire?" He glanced at her again, but didn't say anything. TooSweet took his silence as confirmation. "How you know?" she asked, looking back at the pursuing sedan behind them. "Who the hell are you, anyway?" When he didn't answer, she yelled, "If you don't answer me right now! You can stop this car and let me the fuck out. I got enough problems of my own."

"They still behind us?" he casually asked.

"Yeah they still behind us! You can't shake 'em?"

He looked at her and said, "Sweetheart, you must be tripping. This baby's got three-hundred and twenty-five on tap. You're sitting in a 440 Cuda with a six-pack engine, shaker hood scoop, four speed transmission with pistol grip shifter. She can shake the dry tar from under her wheels if I want her to."

Still watching as the sedan closed in behind them, she quickly warned, "Then you betta' tell this bitch to shake her ass. 'Cause they're right behind us with guns and it look like they 'bout to shoot."

Just before reaching the west side highway. He glanced in the rear-view and threw it in third gears. TooSweet watched as the Cuda pulled away from the sedan as if it had been a fading memory.

"I don't think we have to worry about them anymore," she said, looking at him suspiciously. "Now... who the hell are you and what makes you think they weren't Feds?" She eyed the assault weapon lying on top of the blanket in the back seat and said, "By the way, did you know there's an AK on the back seat?"

"For a minute, thought I had to put in some work. Name Sunny Black. Some call me, Black-Sun. I was sent to protect you."

"By who? Better yet, why would someone think I needed to be protected? If those fake ass Fed. wanted to do something to me, they had plenty of opportunity back there in the car."

"By whom," he felt the need to correct her. "Trust me, sweetheart. They woulda' eventually gotten around to it. They were probably hoping you would lead them to your friends."

"My friends? Why? Who the hell were those men?"

He looked at her and asked, "You know 'bout the trade- off?"

"Me for the disk. Yeah. Why?"

7

"I work for SunRise now. His boy, Tyrone 'pose to be training me to y'all ways."

"SunRise?"

"He sent me to protect you." He briefly looked at her and said, "I guess he thought you needed protecting." He smiled. "Guess he was right."

TooSweet rolled her eyes angrily before asking, "You said Tyrone suppose to be training you. To do what?"

"To learn y'all ways. He had me follow you. That's how I knew those cats in the sedans were following you long before you met up with that old cat you were with at the restaurant." He looked at her with a curiosity and asked, "Did you know he was a cop?" When TooSweet didn't answer, he changed the subject. "After you and the old man stepped into the restaurant and sat down to order. One of those fake Feds made a phone call in a coffee shop down the street from where you and pops ate. I followed and overheard enough of the conversation to know they weren't Feds.

TooSweet looked at him and rolled her eyes, but didn't say anything. She was more confuse now than ever. If SunRise knew where to find me? she silently speculated. Who I was with and what was about to happen? He had to know about my relationship with, Sheets? She then looked at Black-Sun to ask, "What did SunRise tell you?"

"Me? Nothing. I never even met the cat. His boy Tyrone put me on you. Called me yesterday and said SunRise was out of town, but should be back later sometime today. After explaining about the trade-off. He wanted me to keep an eye on you. Make sure everything went smoothly."

"When exactly did you start following me?"

"I had eyes on you since yesterday," he said before continuing. "In light of what just happened, I'd say your boy SunRise is on top of his game, wouldn't you?"

Caught-up in her own thoughts, TooSweet was silent.

"About that disk?" he changed the subject.

"What about it?"

"I'd say those fake Feds work for the man whose name is on it?"

"Johnathen Crain?"

"That could be the name he gave me?"

"Who?"

"Tyrone."

"Are you sure?"

He looked at her. "About the name? No, I'm not. Why? You know him?"

"No, but my lawyer does. They tried to arrest me for two bodies, but before the police had a chance to take me down town...."

"Those fake G-Men showed," he interrupted. "I know. I was there, remember?"

"Then you also know they dropped me off two blocks from where I was arrested. My lawyer was waiting for me. He told me my people traded me for a computer disk that..." Before TooSweet could finish, he interrupt her again.

"You know what was on it?"

"I personally never got a chance to check it out. I suspect a lot of names, transaction, incriminating shit, you know." She looked at him for conformation. Once she realized he wasn't offering any. She asked and answered her own question. "Did Tyrone mention what we represent? It's an anti drug organization called, FOLD?"

"He didn't have to. I got that from the people who ultimately convinced me to accept SunRise's invitation into your FOLD. He sounds like one of the good guys. Can't wait to meet him."

"Then I guess he didn't tell you we interrupted a shit-load of cocaine in Queens that was about to be distributed throughout the east coast. That's where we found the disk. As a retiring gift, I gave the drug-bust to some ass-hole who I thought was my friend. "

"That wouldn't happen to be the elderly gentleman you were having dinner with, would it?" TooSweet looked at him angrily but didn't

10

reply only because she knew he was being an ass-hole. "What I don't understand is, if you and that old 'cat were suppose to be friends. Why would he cross you like that? Unless, of course he was down with those fake G-men?"

"I don't know how he could have been. He didn't know anything about the disk. I guess he was just being a cop."

"Okay. Maybe he wasn't down with those fake-ass G-men, but you and I both know that doesn't let him off the hook. As far as your lawyer is concerned. It really looks like he was the one who ultimately crossed you. And if that's true? They probably knows everything about you and your friends."

"You sure do a lot of speculating, don't you?"

"One and one is two all day long, sweetheart. What kind of legal aid did y'all hire?" Without waiting for an answer, he continued. "It don't matter. He's probably dead by now anyway. They damn sure don't need him anymore. If he's still alive, he'll definitely be dead by tonight." He paused briefly before continuing. "Let me ask you something. Do you by any chance know if SunRise made copies of that disk?"

"I'm almost positive 'Rise had someone make a copy. They fucking with the wrong crew now."

"You a'ight?"

TooSweet did not answer. Caught up in her own thoughts, she began rambling, "That piece of shit told me he gave the disk to the D.A., but they couldn't prosecute without hurting a lot of other people whose name wasn't even on the disk. People like the so-call judge who suppose to have signed the federal warrant that granted me immunity. Who the hell is this guy, Crain? And who the hell is his father suppose to be?"

He looked at her briefly and smiled. "You believed him?"

"At the time, I didn't have any reason not to," she said. Adding, "If those men weren't really federal agents. If they worked for the man on the disk and my dumb ass attorney gave them the disk. We're in a shit load of trouble?"

"Not if y'all made a copy." He reminded her. When TooSweet didn't confirm, he looked at her and asked, "You do have a copy, right? You just told me you did?"

"Yeah. There's suppose to be, if Joey ever got around to it?"

He frowned in frustration. "You mean to tell me you don't know for sure?" While he waited for an answer. TooSweet noticed something in his voice that told her to proceed with caution. Realizing she probably said too much already. She tried to change the subject.

"Where we going?"

"Back to Paterson. Right now, you and your friends have a bounty on y'all heads. SunRise knows this. Which was why he brought me in.

Eventually this Crain person will find a way to get to you. The only thing that might save you and your friends is leverage. The only leverage worth anything to them is a copy of that disk. Without it, those people will not stop. There is no running, or hiding. Thanks to your lawyer, they now have Intel. files on you and everyone in your crew your lawyer knew about. Of course they won't stop there. Every relative, every friend, acquaintance, are all in danger."

He was beginning to scare her. "Why the hell did SunRise bring you in? You suppose to save the day, or some shit?"

"I suspect he heard about the type of cat I use to be. A lot of things sure have changed since I've been gone."

"Where you from?"

"It's not important."

"It is to me."

"The important thing was me getting to you before they did." TooSweet was silent. He could see that she didn't really trust him. "Look," he tried to reassure her. "I know you have a lot of questions. Ones that I really can't answer. I'm sure SunRise will fill you in when you see him."

Caught up in her own thoughts, she didn't know what to think.

He saw the confused look on her face an said, "I know this might be a lot for you to digest all at once, but SunRise obviously understand what he's up against. These people are not gonna' stop looking for you, your friends, or the copy of the disk. If, that is, there is one. Whatever y'all have, or had, threatens them. That makes you a threat. The only way to ensure their safety is to eliminate the threat. That means pushing you, your attorney, and anyone else who might have saw the information on the disk. They could do it without anyone asking any questions. Look how easy it was for them to fake federal credentials and assume custody over you. It's not easy to fake government documents that would fool a trained detective, but they did. Unless, of course your friend, the one who arrested you is also working for them? Shit ain't no joke. You and your crew ain't just threatening some drug dealer and their drug money. Y'all fucking with executives and dirty corporate capital. They play for keeps." He paused briefly before stating in no uncertain term, "If we lose, we're dead. Ain't no coming back from that."

TooSweet had to admit. Everything he was saying made sense. Still, deep down she wondered if she could really trust the man who went by the name, Sunny Black. She had recently put her faith in truth in someone she thought to be a friend and got burnt. She looked at him and whined, "What you think we should do?"

"My orders were to take you at my place until we hear from SunRise. He suppose to be back sometime today," he said without looking at her.

Delighted about his newly acquired wealth. Melvin Vincent was counting his finder's fee when he heard a noise. At first, he thought it might be his wife's live-in nurse and called out to her. "Rosa? Rosa, is that you?" When no one answered, he immediately suspected something was wrong. He quickly placed the money back into the case. Sat the case under his desk and got up to look outside the office door. "Rosa, is that you?" he all but shout. Again, no one answered. He began to worry that something was really wrong and immediately headed up stairs to check on his wife. As Vincent eased up the steps, he felt a presence behind him. He slowly turned around and saw an intruder pointing a gun at him. He immediately recognized the intruder and said a silent prayer for his wife with hopes that she would be spared. "CLACK! CLACK!"

# NEMESIS III

# CHAPTER 2

Tyrone had been instructed by SunRise to meet him at the apartment. Instead of finding SunRise. BeeBop, who had also been given the same instructions, greeted him at the door. The first to arrive, she had been lounging in the front room watching a football game. Dolphins verses the Cowboys. "Who's winning?" he asked. Not because he was into the game. Aside from him trying to be sociable, it just seemed like the first appropriate question to ask. Truth be told, sports was never really his thing. The Olympics, maybe. That is, women's track and field. Sometimes even gymnastics, but that was the extent of it.

"You mean who won. This game is over," she replied before turning the television off.

"Well... who won, baby girl?"

"Miami pushed them by two. You heard from 'Rise, too?" she had to ask. It would have been Tyrone's second question, but he allowed her to beat him to it. It was from both of their understanding SunRise wanted to talk with them about something very important.

"Yeah." He glanced at his watch. "Actually, I thought he'd be here by now?"

"He say what it was about?" Before BeeBop got an answer, they both heard a key slid in the door. When the door opened, SunRise stepped in, alone. Both BeeBop and Tyrone stood.

"Hey, 'Rise," They greeted in unison.

Once BeeBop realized Robin wasn't with him. She immediately asked, "Where's Robin?"

"On her way out of the country. Something came up that commanded her immediate attention." He lied in an effort to spare them the anxiety of the truth. The truth was, there was a storm coming, and they were all caught in the middle of it. BeeBop did not question his explanation, but the look on her face clearly conveyed disbelief. He had anticipate as much. BeeBop was anything, but naive and he really hated insulting her intelligence. He knew she trusted him without question and whatever reason he gave was either the truth, or he had a good reason for giving it.

"Well..." she began by giving him a full hug.".. I'm glad you're home."

"So am I, Bop," he admitted before coming straight to the point. "We have a problem, which is why I called this meeting."

"What's up, 'Rise?" Tyrone asked with obvious concern. SunRise casually took off his top coat and laid it over the back of the white leather recliner before taking a seat next to them.

"Bop? Where's the copy of that disk I asked you to have Joey make?"

"I didn't get a chance to put it up. It's in your room on top of the dresser."

"Good girl. Now..." he slowly began. "...don't ask me what's going on, because I'm not really sure I know. Be that as it may, we're shutting down as a precautionary measure.

"Shutting down what? The FOLD? Why?" BeeBop all but shouted.

"Claim down, Bop. It's just a precautionary measure."

"Precautionary measure to what?" she asked.

SunRise stood, walked over to the window and gazed out into the night.

"What's going on, 'Rise?" she pressed for an explanation.

He slowly turned to face her. "Without going into any detail. I have reason to believe the FOLD has been compromised. As a result, we're all in danger."

"What kind of danger?" BeeBop asked, more concern now than ever.

"Does it matter?" he took a quick peek at his watch before walking back over to the recliner to sit again. "Has anyone heard from 'Sweet?"

Both BeeBop and Tyrone looked at one another before answering, no.

"Last I heard," said BeeBop, "she was suppose to be having dinner with an old friend in Harlem. But I already told you that over the phone." She then looked at Tyrone. Wondering if he had heard anything from TooSweet.

SunRise rubbed his jaws while also looking at Tyrone.

"I took care of that, 'Rise. I talked to Mr. Vincent right after the trade took place. You were right about her friend. Luckily everything worked out in our favor. I don't know where she could be now. When I talked to Vincent, he said he left her hours ago?"

"Who said they left her hours ago?" BeeBop quickly asked. She hated being left in the dark. When both men ignored her question, she did not press the issue.

SunRise stood and grabbed his coat. He reached into the inside pocket and pulled out an envelope. He then looked directly at BeeBop. "This envelopes contain enough money for you, Joey and the children to go under for a while."

"GO UNDER!" she repeated in protest before adding "And do what?" She had hoped SunRise would give her some kind of sensible explanation. Instead, he just handed her the envelop. "What the hell is going on, 'Rise?" Her tone was becoming more and more anxious for answers. When SunRise walked off into the back room, she looked at Tyrone for answers.

"Don't look at me, baby-girl. I'm just as in the dark as you. You know how 'Rise is. Don't wanna' say anything until he have all the facts.

When it's safe to come back, he'll send word. For now, just do as you were told. You, Joey and the children have to go under. I hear the southwest is nice this time of year."

BeeBop completely understood what he meant. As much as she would have liked more answers, she knew none would be forth coming. "How much time do you think we have before leaving and how long do we have to stay?" she quietly asked while avoiding eye contact with him.

"That information I don't have, Bop. I wish I could tell you more... but...."

"Well can you at least tell me what exactly took place at Michael Henderson's house that night?"

"Good question, 'Bop,'" said SunRise while re-entering the room. He looked at Tyrone and said, "I want to know everything that happened from your point of view. What you saw, what you felt, what type of action you took and why?"

Tyrone thought about it, "Well," he said as he carefully began to elaborate the events that led up to Vicki's injuries, and her husband's demise. "I did what you asked me to do. Go see Black-Sun. Afterwards, I followed our people to Henderson's house. By the time I realized what was happening, it was about to go down. I saw the girl, Vicki go up to the house first. Her husband, Londell stayed outside the car timing her. At least that was my impression because he kept looking at his watch. When she arrive at the front door, she rung the bell. When the door opened, she appeared either confused, or

21

surprised. Maybe a little of both. I never saw who actually answered the door. Vicki later told me it was a white woman about her age with blond hair. Except for the age thing, it fits the description of Henderson's wife. Anyway... a few more minutes went by and I noticed the young boy, her husband becoming impatient. Maybe even worried, or both. About five minutes later, he rushed up the concrete steps that led to the front door. I must have blinked because the next thing I knew, Vicki was coming out. From the look on her husband's face, I knew something was wrong. That's when she collapsed in his arms right outside the house." Tyrone took a brief moment to defend his position. "I couldn't make a move without blowing my cover."

"What happened next, Tye?" SunRise calmly urged him on.

"The kid eased her down and surveyed the perimeter without going into the house. He must of thought all was clear because he tucked his gun and was about to pick her up when some middle aged pencil-neck in a suit wearing glasses came out of the house and walked right up on him. Before the kid even realized he was in danger. Pencil-neck had his gun to baby-boy's head. By the time baby-boy looked up, pencil-neck busted off on him point-blank range. That's when I got out of the car to light his ass up.

While I was creeping up on pencil-neck, he must have realized Vicki was still alive. I knew he was about to finish her off. So I took aim and was about to squeeze off when all of a sudden, he fell over on top of baby-boy. I didn't realize he was dead until I got closer."

"I thought you pushed him, Tye?" said BeeBop.

"Wasn't me. Someone from inside the house pushed him. A single shot right between the eyes." He paused briefly with a puzzled look on his face. "I just thought about something that didn't hit me before."

"What?" both BeeBop and SunRise immediately asked.

"I didn't remember hearing any shots being fired. Whoever shot from inside, used a silencer. I wasn't about to make the same mistake baby-boy made. So I went inside to check it out. The first thing I saw was a .45 lying on the floor in the foyer. I didn't touch it, or anything. I just moved a little deeper into the house. That's when I spotted three of Mike's boys in the living-room sitting in front of a wide screen. Dead than-a-muthafucka'. Looked like they were poisoned, or choked to death. They had white foam around their mouths. It was ugly." Tyrone paused again as if he had just thought of something else. "You know... I could of sworn I heard a door from within the house closing. I was about to check it out when I heard the girl moaning. I backed out the house, checked her wounds. It was a through in through. Baby-boy and his assassin were both dead. I checked pencil-neck's ID, grabbed the girl and headed for the safe house on North Main. After I got there, I called Doc., and had him meet me there. He arrived shortly after and patched her up. That was that."

"Let me ask you something," SunRise began. "Do you think Michael Henderson shot the assassin from inside the house? If I'm not mistaken, you never said anything about the actual target, or did I miss something?"

"I Honestly don't know, 'Rise. I didn't see his body and never got around to ask her about him. All the shit she's been through? I never found the appropriate time. Personally, I don't think it was Henderson. I think it was another hitter. If Henderson's boys got it like that, I'm almost certain Henderson got it, too."

"What did Doc say?" asked BeeBop.

"He said she was gonna' be just fine. He said something about some swelling and abrasions to her jaw. Probably the result of a scuffle. He didn't think it was broken, or anything. It could have been fractured, but without X-rays, there was no way of really knowing."

"Where is she now?" asked SunRise.

"At her mother-in-law's. She left a few hours after Doc patched her up. I'm not sure, but I think her mother-in-law stays on West Broadway. I think baby-girl blames herself for her partner's death."

"I noticed during your account, you never said anything about her version of what happen?" SunRise took the time to pointed out.

That's because she didn't give one. As a Matter of fact, she hardly said anything. Except she wanted to be with her mother-in-law. I guess she wanted to be the one to break the news to her mother-in-law? You know, help each other get through the kid's death."

BeeBop thought for a moment. "She might be the only one who can tell us what went wrong? We have to talk to her, 'Rise."

SunRise looked at her and said, "What you have to do is round your little ready-made family up and be on the first thing smoking as you were ordered. Let me do what I do."

"I'm serious, 'Rise. Joey told me who is was. You know what she did?" BeeBop asked him.

"Fortunately, yes."

"Then you know she ain't hardly finish. She might need our help, Rise? You know she just ain't gonna' let it go."

Tyrone quickly spoke up, "You, Joey and the kids get the hell out of town as you were told," saving SunRise the trouble of repeating himself.

"And what about you, Tye? What you gonna' do, stay?"

"As I am told, Bop." He stood and put on his coat. "Be careful, 'Rise."

"Always," said SunRise before asking, "What's the deal with Black-Sun?"

"I had him check that club out. I also explained how important it was for him to try and find out as much as he could about that young-boy, Teflon. I also made sure he understood that 'Sweet's situation took priority." He glanced at BeeBop before walking over to SunRise. "Don't worry," he tried to speak without arising the suspicion of BeeBop. "I gave him all the details and a photo of both parties in question so he'd know who he was tracking."

"What happen at the club?" SunRise asked.

"As far as I know, not much. Black-Sun told me Teflon was there sweating some dancer. The good news is, he knows the dancer Teflon was sweating from back in the day. He said she offered to cut into Teflon for him, but he didn't want to involve her."

"You think he can get her to work with us?"

"I'll have to get back with you on that one. I haven't heard from him since."

"Good work, Tye. I'll talk to you later."

"A'ight, 'Rise." Tyrone looked at BeeBop and smiled. "Stay safe and take care of Joey and the kids. We'll keep a close watch on Wendi. You know, make sure she gets the help she needs."

"I almost forgot to tell you they have a bed for her at, Straight & Narrow. As long as she wants help, she'll get it," BeeBop said while standing to walk Tyrone to the door.

Before he left, he looked her straight in the eyes and said, "Remember, never break protocol." She smiled, kissed him on the cheek and watched as he casually walked down the hall.

After closing the door, she turned to face SunRise. Who was now hanging his coat in the closet. When he walked off towards the back room, she quickly asked, "Where you going?"

"To formulate a plan." he said without bothering to stop.

26

BeeBop followed close behind. "Not before you tell me who, or what got you so spooked? And who the hell is this Black-Sun y'all keep talking about?"

When SunRise abruptly stopped to confront her, she almost ran directly into him. "You have your orders, Bop," he said, leaving her standing in the hall while he stepped into the bathroom closing the door behind him.

"Well how we 'pose to reach you? And what about 'Sweet?"

"You know the rules," he yelled through the door. "You don't. 'Sweet can take care of herself." He hated not being truthful with her but it was necessary.

After leaving Robin at the property in South Jersey where she would be safe. The first thing he did upon arriving in town, was stop at Black-Sun's apartment. Once TooSweet and Black-Sun filled him in on what was going on, he ordered Black-Sun to make sure TooSweet made it to a FOLD safe-house in Arizona.

He thought about Robin and was sure he had done the right thing. The contents of what they found in the envelop marked, CONFIDENTIAL at Rossi's antique shop was more disturbing then what they could have ever imagined.

As promised, SunRise personally delivered the envelop to Rossi's attorney in Cape May County. And because it was much too dangerous to have copies made. He photo copied the contents before delivering the envelop to the attorney.

BeeBop slowly turned and walked back into the front room. She was about to leave when SunRise opened the bathroom door, stuck his head out and yelled, "Yo, Bop!"

"Yeah?"

"This place never existed,"

She did not reply. There was no need to. She already knew what he meant. If he wasn't setting up another spot for them to meet? He was terminating the FOLD. A move she found to be a little extreme.

After putting on her coat, she reached into the pocket for her keys. Unhooked the spare to the apartment from her key-ring. Then carefully placed it in clear view on top of the end-table. She was about to leave when she thought of something. "Oh, yeah. Can't forget this." she muttered while walking over to the glass-top coffee table to retrieve the envelop SunRise had given her earlier. Once it was safely tucked in the inside pocket of her coat. She took one last look around the small apartment she often called her second home, then left.

SunRise knew his plate was full. His only lead was a combination of information he received from Robin, Tyrone Sharp, Black-Sun, and TooSweet. Apparently, Johnathen Crain Junior was trying to clean house. It would appear, the Dominicans from the house in Queens were the first to go. Michael Henderson was the second, and Melvin Vincent would probably be next if he wasn't dead already? BeeBop had been right about one thing, he concluded as he stood under the hot water that flowed freely from the shower-head above him. Vicki was far from done. Still, his main concern was for her safety. As good as he knew she was, she was hardly prepared for who she was about to go up against.

He thought about the lawyer in Cape May Court House. The people who paid him to hire Robin's father, Rossi to steal that information would have no problem murdering to retrieve it. SunRise knew it was just a matter of time before the lawyer gave his clients Robin's name. Which was why he wasted no time getting the envelop to the lawyer with hopes of satisfying all parties connected.

He thought about the woman he peeped leaving the lawyer's office with the envelop ninety minutes after he delivered it. She was slim, white, middle age and well dressed. He wasn't sure if she was the actual client Rossi's lawyer spoke of, or just a carrier? Which was why he followed her. A pursuit that led him to Cape May airport where he watched as she boarded a small plain. He later learned the plain was a charter that arrived from and returned to New York. He had no idea who the woman was or what roll she played if any?

# NEMESIS III

# CHAPTER 3

Londell's funeral was held on a Saturday. Ma'Matty and Vicki were extremely surprised to see so many people turn up at the vigil, and even more at the funeral. Vicki knew some of the people who came to paid their respects. She also knew the majority of them only knew Londell by reputation. That was fine with her. One of the many things Londell had taught her was, strength will always respect strength.

There were also a host of attractive, young females who took Londell's death very hard. Vicki suspected they were groupies left over from his unauthorized fan-club. At the viewing, Vicki actually overheard one of the girls brag to her friends, "I finally got to kiss those big ass lips on Face's fine ass," as he laid to rest in his casket. Londell was the type of man who never thought between his legs. He either liked you, or he didn't. A sentiment that came from the heart.

Amongst the many of those who paid their respects were seasoned killers. Other had been up and coming hoods who gravitated towards the money. Which, for them, was in the murder game. She even saw SunRise, who was someone she did not expect to see. There were also a few new faces from out of town who came to pay their respects. Vicki assumed Londell had 'put in work' for them some time during his past.

Several 'old-heads' in the game offered to help Vicki exact the proper revenge on her husband's murderers, but Vicki graciously declined. One old-head in particular who claimed Londell had been like a little brother to him, was adamant about going after the people responsible.

"And you are?" Vicki curiously asked the slim built, middle aged, dark-skinned man with the droopy eyes.

"Bilaal Bonds, but everyone calls me, Ghost. You might of heard him mention me?" The name did ring a bell in Vicki's head, but she couldn't remember Londell ever mentioning him to her.

"Oh, yeah. I do remember him mentioning you," she lied.

"Sorry for your lost, but like I said, if you need me in any way, shape, or form, I ain't hard to find."

Vicki smiled politely before walking away.

"I'm staying on Governor," he shouted behind her. "Just ask for Ghost."

Vicki kept walking. She never placed too much trust in people who calls themselves friends. In her experience, a friend will betray you quicker than a sworn enemy out of envy alone. Besides, she had seen enough bloodshed to last a life-time. For her, the murder game died with her husband. At least that's what she kept telling herself. She was kind of hoping if she said it enough times, she would actually start believing it. But deep down, she knew nothing was ever that simple.

Throughout the funeral, she had been strong. Taking her lost on the chin. But at the burial her sorrow got the best of her.

As they began lowering the casket into the ground, Vicki suddenly realized Londell was gone and she was never going to see him again. She tried to fight the pain, but out of nowhere, her lips began to tremble as tears swelled up in her eyes and ran down the side of her face even before she blinked. Having established a reputation for showing no emotions. No one had expected the woman known as, 'Nemesis' to take death itself so hard. Yet, everyone clearly understood. Vicki dropped to her knees and screamed at the top of her lungs over and over again, "DON'T LEAVE ME, BABY! PLEASE! PLEASE! COME BACK! COME BAAAACK!" while pounding her tightly clinched fist onto the soft soil. It was the second time she had been visibly overwhelmed by sorrow. The first time was about a year ago. Londell had been grazed in the head by a bullet that knocked him unconscious. Vicki was sure he had been killed, but Londell woke and found her racing aimlessly down the street in his car while muttering incoherently to herself.

As Ma'Matty tried to comfort her, others assisted. One particular individual was a tall, heavy-set, light-skinned man in his early forties who sported long, rope-like dreadlocks that hung to the small of his back. Vicki couldn't help noticing the man was a spitting image of a man she once met by the name of, Baxter Keys. A man Londell murdered over a year ago. He was also the reason Vicki quickly managed to get a hold of herself and remained on the alert for possible impending danger. What actually happened between Londell and Baxter Keys made her realize Londell had just as many enemies as he had friends. And because she didn't personally know everyone who came to pay their respects. She had every reason to believe, amongst his friends may lie foe.

Hours after the funeral, Vicki and Ma'Matty sat quietly in the front room. Ma'Matty sat on one end of the sofa humming a spiritual hymn while putting the final alterations on a sweater she had been knitting for Vicki.

Vicki however, had descended into a deep state of depression. Curled up at the other end of the sofa wearing a pair of Londell's old pajamas. She stared aimlessly at an old photograph of Londell that hung on the wall across the room. It was a graduation portrait shot taken some years ago when Londell graduated from grade school. He couldn't have been no more than thirteen years of age in the photo and even then, he didn't smile.

Ma'Matty stood, walked over to Vicki and handed her the sweater she had just finished knitting. "Here, baby. Try it on." Vicki reluctantly stood, took the sweater and tried it on. She never thought she would even like it, more less expect it to actually fit. But it did and she really liked it. Ma'Matty smiled and told her to turn around. Vicki slowly turned while looking down at the sweater on her. The black knitted mock-neck was a tight fit, but there was plenty of room to support her large D-cups.

"Perfect fit," said Ma'Matty. "You like it?"

Finally managing a genuine smile, Vicki quietly replied, "Yeah. It's nice. Thanks, Ma'."

Ma'Matty helped Vicki out of the sweater and thought how nice it was seeing Vicki smile again. She had hoped it would last, but after they were both seated again Ma'Matty looked at Vicki and saw the same sad expression Vicki had been previously wearing since the funeral. She knew Vicki had been through a lot this last past week. They both have. Ma' also knew from a life-time of experience, time heals all wounds and this too shall pass. "Vicki, baby, you look tired. You been sitting here on the sofa next to me all evening. Why don't you go get some rest. We going to services in the morning, okay?"

"Okay, Ma'" Vicki slowly stood, walked over to Ma'Matty and lightly kissed her on the cheek. "Goodnight, Ma'."

Ma'Matty smiled and said, "Sleep well, baby."

That night, Vicki laid on top of the covers in the small bedroom Londell had grew up in and stared into the dark at the ceiling. The harder she tried not to think about Londell, the more lonely she felt. The thought of never seeing him, touching him, or hearing his voice again was becoming too overwhelming for her to bear. Her eyes began to burn as they filled with tears and began to run down the side of her face. She turned over on her side and silently wept herself to sleep.

"You know, baby," Ma'Matty began as she sat on the edge of the small bed beside Vicki. "Everything happens for a reason. God doesn't give us anything we can't handle. He brought us into this world to fulfill a purpose in life. We each have one. Once that purpose is completed, we move on." Vicki did not believe that for one minute. She knew Ma'Matty was just trying to make her feel better. Strangely enough, it worked. "You should go out and get some air. It ain't right, pretty young woman like yourself stuck in this stuffy old place all day. I know you loved him, baby. I loved him, too. He was my purpose in life, and you, his.' She smiled at Vicki and said, "Don't you worry one bit. Your purpose will find you. But you making it hard if you don't move on with your life."

"How can I? He was all I had," Vicki heard herself saying.

"In time baby, you will and your purpose will become clear."

Sound asleep in the comfort of his bed; Asmar was abruptly awaken by a chill. He look over at the window and noticed it was open. Just as he was about to get out of bed to close it, he began hearing a strange, irritating sound. Still laying in the same position, he tried to identify the noise, but couldn't. He rolled over onto his back and looked around without moving his head, but saw nothing out of the ordinary. He sat up on his elbows and listened. The sound had abruptly ceased. Without giving it too much thought, he decided to leave the window open. As he tried to drift back off to sleep, he began hearing the creepy noise again. "What the fuck!" he angrily blurted while reaching for a night-light over the head of his bed. Before he had a chance to clicked on the light, his heart skipped a beat when he saw a man standing in the corner of his room. "Oh shit!" he immediately reach for his gun, but froze when he felt the cold nuzzle of someone's gun pressed against the cheek of his face. "What the...."

"We talked to Punchie today. She was a little upset with me. Why the fuck would she think we peeled her for her end of the Spivey job?"

After realizing the man holding the gun to his head and doing all the talking was Bomani Africa, and the man standing in the shadow of his room was Ghost. He angrily whispered, "What the fuck you crazy-ass-fools doing in my bedroom? Y'all must have lost your minds rolling up on me like you crazy!"

Just answer the question!" shouted Ghost.

"Hold your voice down, yo'! If you take that gun out of my face, I'll explain."

The moment Bomani lowered his weapon, Ghost cocked his nine and aimed it at Asmar's head.

"Talk fast, yo'. We ain't got all night," said Bomani.

"If you check that bottom drawl over there," Asmar pointed to the dresser across the room. "You should find a paper bag with that lil bitch's name on it."

Bomani nodded to Ghost, who immediately found the brown paper bag just where Asmar said it would be. He then looked inside and counted it. After nodding to Bomani, confirming it was all there, both men put their weapons away.

"Really, yo'?" Asmar began. "You actually think a joker like me would beat my own cousin? Y'all got the game twisted." Asmar took a moment to breathe a sigh of relief before continuing, "I can't believe you two fools rolled up on me while I was asleep. And at my Grandmother's, Bee?"

"What was the hold up getting shortie her stack?" asked Ghost.

"Bee, man," Asmar ignored ghost and directed his explanation to Bomani. "I ain't seen that lil' bitch." He then looked at Ghost and said with a nervous half smile, "It ain't like she wasn't gonna' get paid."

The two men stared at Asmar with cold, suspicious eyes before leaving the same way they had entered, through the window.

"You two old ass jokers just tell that crazy ass bitch I said, fuck her!" After he was sure they were gone, he got out of bed to close and lock the window. "And fuck you, too."

Punchie was waiting in the back seat when the two men got back into the car. "Here you go, young soldier," Bomani said while tossing the bag over his shoulder in Punchie's lap.

As soon as Punchie looked inside, her eyes grew in disbelief. "Oh, shit!," she shouted excitedly. "Um' rich!"

"Not quite lil' soldier, but if you keep throwing us work like the last joker you gave us? You will be."

"Shit. I know this guy we can hit up righ' now. Young joker that stay in the C.C.P. I don't know how he getting it, but he be holding like Fort Knock, you feel me."

"What's his name?" Ghost immediately asked.

"Go by the name, SunRise. Every time I see that joker he got it on. Flossin' like a mufucka', you feel me."

"We gonna' pass on that one, but if you come up with something we can use, holla, you heard?"

"I heard, but um' telling you right now, Asmar is out. Family or no family. That joker shady, you feel me?"

"When it comes to that cake," Commented Ghost. "who ain't. Where can we drop you?"

"Right here, you feel me. I'll see y'all when I see you," she said while exiting the car, but stopped when she thought of something she almost forgot to mention. "Oh yeah. I heard some Jamaican running 'round town asking about that fool, Spivey. My man told me he heard they offering a ten piece for info', you heard?"

"How they look?" asked Bomani.

"Wreak said the joker doing all the talking was some tall, dark skin lame with long thick-ass dreads like yours. Be careful, yo'. Joker 'pose to be rolling with two other fools, you heard?"

"We heard. Good looking out."

"You know how we get down. Peace!" Punchie quickly got out of the car and hurried off up the street.

Ghost pulled off in the opposite direction. As he drove, he looked at Bomani and asked him why he chose to passed on Punchie's new mark'?"

"It's a bad idea," was Bomani's only reply.

"Why? He balling, ain't he?"

Without looking at Ghost. He said, "That depends on what you mean by balling. He then looked at Ghost and asked, "Any thoughts on the Jamaicans she mentioned?"

"No. You?"

"Naw'."

"What about the mark?"

"We gonna' pass."

"Why?"

"I saw the brotha'. We both did. He ain't hustling," said Bomani. The truth was, he had checked SunRise out after seeing him in the lobby of the C.C.P waiting on the elevator with his lady friend. He could see why Punchie would have pegged SunRise for a baller. Although he had to admit, the young boy did appear to be doing his thing. However, what he remembered about SunRise most was the fact he never avoided making eye contact with him. Most men often avoided Bomani's gaze. SunRise, on the other hand, didn't even blink. Bomani smiled to himself when he thought about it again and realized it was he who conceded first.

He thought about the attractive young female that stood at SunRise's side. He remembered how tightly she clung to the young boy's arm. He also remembered the expensive, dirty coat she was wearing. At the time, he just assumed the young boy was a pimp who had just dragged the dime-piece through the street. That is, until Asmar told him differently.

Vicki woke in a puddle of sweat. The dream she had last night was like no other she had ever experienced. As a matter of fact, what she had dreamt seemed so real, she actually questioned whether it was in fact a dream, or a conversation she actually had with Ma'Matty last night.

Anxious to share the details of her dream with Ma'. She quickly jumped out of bed and slipped out of the wet pajama until she stood completely nude. She then took the damp pajama top and bottom, balled them up and tossed them on top of the bed. Next, she removed the damp sheets and pillow-casing and stuffed everything into the damp pillow-case. She was about to leave the room when it dawned on her she was completely nude. She quickly slipped on a house-robe and headed across the hall to the bathroom with the pillow-case of soiled linen.

Inside the bathroom, she placed the soil linen into the hamper and walked over to the large mirror that hung over the sink. As she stood there staring at her reflection, she thought about her dream and could still remembered every little detail. Which was in itself, unusual. Normally she was only able to remember bits and pieces of something she had dreamt. And even then the bits and pieces she remembered often made very little sense. What made this particular one different, she had no idea?

After splashing some cold water on her face. She brushed her teeth, then ran the shower before heading back to the bedroom to retrieve her underclothes and a few other items. Before leaving the bedroom, she caught a glimpse of her watch on top of the dresser. It was after ten. She couldn't believe she had over slept. More importantly, why Ma' hadn't waken her in time for services? She dismissed her concerns, rationalizing that Ma' probably decided to let her sleep and went off to services alone.

During Vicki's shower, she couldn't stop thinking about Londell. She thought about the funeral and all the faces she remembered seeing. She thought about SunRise, it was nice of him to pay his respects. She knew he wanted to talk with her but had too much class to bring up business at such a time.

She thought some more about Londell and all the offers she received at the funeral to help her retaliate against those responsible for his murder. She thought about taking them up on their offers, but in her heart she was not really feeling it. Without the love of her life, she just didn't see the point.

She stepped out of the shower and began to dry. While grooming, she was surprised she no longer felt depressed. She thought about what Ma' had said in her dream last night and for some reason, it made her feel better about life in general.

On her way back to the bedroom, she noticed something very odd. Ma'Matty's bedroom door was closed. The only time Ma' closed her bedroom-door was when she was either retiring for the night, dressing, or undressing. Vicki found something else odd? Ma' would never miss a service. Especially after what they had been through.

After dressing, Vicki walked up to the door and knocked a few times. "Ma'?" she called out, but there was no response. As she slowly opened the door and peeked in, Ma'Matty was lying in bed and appeared to be sleeping peacefully. "Ma', if you going to services, it's after ten?" When Ma'Matty did not wake, Vicki knew something was wrong. She slowly approached the old woman's bed-side and called out, "Ma'?" her voice cracked as she began to fear the worse. "MA'! she lightly shook the old woman. When Ma' didn't respond, Vicki knew in her heart the old woman was gone. As her eyes filled with tears, she became frantic. "MA'! MA'!" she shouted over and over again. "PLEASE! WAKE UP! WAKE UP!" PLEASE...PLEASE...DON'T YOU LEAVE ME, TOO! WAKE-UP! PLEASE! WAKE-UUUUUP!" her voice trailed off into a series of uncontrollable sobs. Vicki dropped to her knees beside the bed and buried her face in the old woman's chest. Ma'Matty had peacefully passed away in her sleep last night. Leaving Vicki all alone to find her purpose in life.

Vicki cried so hard, the neighbors called the landlady. Because the sound of mourning came from Ma'Matty's apartment. The landlady had just assumed the family was grieving from the lost of Londell. The last thing she wanted was to intrude at such a time. That is, until Mr. Willie came by. When Ma'Matty never showed up at church, or phoned in. Mr. Willie, an old family friend and deacon of the church, immediately suspected something was wrong and had the landlady let him into the apartment. When they heard sobbing coming from one of the bedrooms, they walked in and found Ma'Matty lying in bed. Vicki was curled up on the bed in a fetus position beside her, weeping. Though it was obvious that Ma'Matty had passed away. Mr. Willie checked her vitals, then called the ambulance. When the Medical Technicians tried to move the body, Vicki became violent and had to be restraint and sedated.

At one point, Vicki swore to find the people responsible for murdering her husband and make them pay, but something happened that changed her heart. It was her mother-in-law, the Reverend Matty Dixson who made Vicki realize something that could not be articulated, just intuitively understood. Now that Ma' was gone. Vicki found herself all alone just as she was the day she first arrived in Paterson, New Jersey.

# CHAPTER 4

Held overnight for observation, Vicki was released with a clean bill of health the next morning.

While being wheeled out of the hospital still wearing the very same clothing she had been wearing when she was first admitted. The early winter breeze made its presence know with temperatures at a freezing twenty nine degrees. The nurse who had wheeled Vicki out of the hospital offered to call her a cab, but Vicki graciously declined. In hindsight, she wished she had taken the nurse up on her offer.

As she began hastily walking, she noticed a young Latino woman leaning up against a white on white Nissan watching her. At least that's what her instincts told her, but she really couldn't be sure. Dressed in white leather pant and matching jacket, the woman wore a pair of dark designer shades that made it impossible for anyone to see her eyes. For all Vicki knew, the woman could have been eyeing someone in her direction. Ultimately Vicki decided she was probably just being paranoid and dismissed her concerns altogether. That is, until she noticed the woman approaching. "Vicki, right?" the woman asked. Vicki stopped. Her first thoughts were, SunRise had sent the woman to collect her. She knew he probable wanted to see her about what had happen at Henderson's house the night she lost her husband. She just thought he could have had the decency to show up himself.

"Do I know you?" Vicki asked, waiting for the woman to mention SunRise's name.

"I'm Camille LaRue. I heard you were getting out today, so I came to pick you up."

Realizing there is always a probability of danger, Vicki looked at the woman's hands.

The woman noticed and said, "You can relax, I'm actually who I claim to be."

"And who's that?"

"Here to pick you up," she simply answered before continuing. "I was at your mother-in-law's yesterday, but I missed you. I heard about her passing and you have my condolence. Your landlady told me you took her passing kinda' hard. I can understand that. Considering the circumstances," she paused briefly while removing her shades before continuing. "Look, it's kinda' cold out here. Can I drop you someplace? It'll give us a chance to talk."

It was only after the woman removed the dark shades that hid her eyes when Vicki realized there was something about her that seemed very familiar. "About what?"

The woman looked around cautiously. "Have you ever heard of a man by the name of, Johnathen Crain?"

Vicki did not have to think about it. "No. Why?"

"Can we please talk in the car. I'll drop you wherever you wanna' go."

Vicki thought about it and realized she had nowhere to go. "I don't really have any place to go, except back to my mother-in-law's," she held her head down avoiding eye contact.

"If you like," the woman began, "you can stay with me until you figure out what you wanna' do next. I have a suite at the Alexander Hotel on Church street. We can keep one another company. Considering what you've just been through, I really don't think you should be alone." Adept in reading people, the woman took off her white leather jacket and placed it around Vicki's shoulders. She then put her arm around Vicki's waist and guided her to her awaiting car.

"Wait a minute." Vicki stopped short of getting in while staring at the woman suspiciously. "I don't know you! Do I?"

"Not personally, no, but we have met before."

"Really. When? Where?"

"Later. This isn't the time, or place. I'll tell you everything back at my spot, okay?" Without the least bit of resistance, Vicki boarded the vehicle. She wasn't sure why, but for some reason she felt as though she could trust the woman.

As they headed down-town, both woman were silent. Every now and then, the woman would glance at Vicki. Making sure she was all right. Vicki, however, had been preoccupied trying to remember where she had met her, but couldn't. She had just assumed the woman was

Latino, but instead of a Spanish accent, Vicki heard a slight southern slur that was barely noticeable. Ultimately she concluded the woman was probably French descent because of her name. However, it was her swagger that led Vicki to believe the woman probably grew up around blacks. She wanted to ask, but didn't want to appear too forward. There was something very cocky about her, or maybe she was just sure of herself. Vicki thought about the name the woman had threw out there. As far as she knew, she had never heard of anyone by the name of, Johnathen Crain. She began to wonder about the woman's interest in her, and prayed it had nothing to do with her husband's death.

Inside the suite, Vicki stood in the middle of the living area looking around. She had never been in a hotel suite before and was amazed at how large the room actually was. There were gold carpeting throughout the entire suite. "Make yourself at home. I know you gotta' be hungry. I know I am. I'll call room-service and see why they can't whip something up for us. Any special requests?" asked the woman before reaching for the land-line.

"No. Whatever you're having is fine, thank you." Vicki sat on the sofa next to her gracious host and continued to look around the spacious living area. Besides the large sofa and matching coffee table. There was an end-table on the left side of the sofa. Two arm chair faced the thirty-two inch screen television across the room. Up against the wall to Vicki's right sat a small wooden dining table and two wooden chairs. A portion of the bedroom could be seen from where she sat. As far as she could tell, it was almost as big as the living area and also included gold carpeting.

"If you wanna' freshen up," the woman said while hanging up the phone. "the bathroom is right through there," she pointed towards the bedroom. Vicki smiled politely, stood and walked into the bedroom. The bathroom was just off to the left of the bedroom. Vicki however, was in no hurry. Not only was the bedroom enormous, but beautiful as well. Taking the liberty to look around, she tried to imagine what it would cost each week to rent such a suite. To the right there was a queen-size bed. The bed was covered with a beautiful gold bed-spreads. Seven pillows with gold and white striped casings had been strategically placed at the head of the bed.

Equally as beautiful was an antique wooden chair and table stationed in the sitting area near a large window with gold and white curtains.

The woman was still sitting on the sofa when Vicki returned from freshening up. Vicki tried to get a feel of the mysterious woman by studying her facial features, but for some reason she just couldn't figure her out.

"You said something about us meeting before? I don't know why I can't remember?"

"First let me get out of these boots. They're killing my feet," the woman said with a smile. While she began struggling with one of the white, knee-high leather boots, Vicki sat on the sofa next to her. Once the woman realized she probably needed help pulling her boots off. She looked at Vicki and asked if she mind giving her a hand? Vicki hesitated at first before reluctantly getting on one knees to help the woman.

"Thanks," she said after Vicki managed to pull the first on off. "It woulda' taken me forever."

"Maybe I should leave," Vicki suggested.

"I noticed no one was there to pick you up at the hospital?" the woman pointed out.

"I'll be fine," Vicki assured on her way to the door.

"Look, at least have breakfast with me. I've already ordered and there's no way I'll be able to eat it all by myself."

"Thanks," Vicki began, "but I don't know you. I mean, I appreciate the ride and all, but I just don't think ..." Vicki was interrupted by a knock at the door. When the woman opened the door, room-service rolled in the breakfast cart. After tipping the bell-boy, he thanked her and left.

Still standing, Vicki watched as the woman pushed the cart over to the small dining area and began setting the small wooden table.

"Help yourself, I just have to wash my face and hands," said the woman before walking off into the bathroom.

Vicki knew she should have left while she had the chance, but beside the fact she really wanted to hear what the woman had to say, she was famished. The hospital food she was served the night before and this morning was watery and tasteless. The sight and scent of hot-cakes, turkey bacon, and cheese-eggs had her stomach growling.

A few minutes later, the woman returned and found Vicki seated at the small table, but haven't touched anything on the table. Her host, however, sat and began helping herself while insisting Vicki do the same.

As  the two woman ate. Vicki began questioning her.

"You said you wanted to talk to me?

"There's so much to say, I don't know where to begin."

"Why don't you start by telling me how we met? Was it at the funeral?" Vicki asked.

"I was at the funeral, but never had a chance to speak with you. Besides, I didn't think that was the proper time, or place. You know what I mean?" Without waiting for Vicki to reply,  the woman continued. "Originally I'm from New Orleans."

"I've never been to New Orleans?"

"That's not where we met.

"Excuse me," Vicki casually interrupted while wiping her mouth. "but what does where you're from have to do with me? I'm not trying to be impolite. I mean, I just lost my family and don't even know where I'm going, or what I'm going to do next." Vicki irritably tossed the cloth napkin on top of the table and stood. "Don't get me wrong, I appreciate the ride and food, but I don't have time to sit here and listen to you ramble about where you're from."

"If you give me a minute, I'll explain everything. Who I am, how we met, everything."

"So far, you haven't," Vicki found herself becoming angry and frustrated while turning to leave.

The woman leaned back in her chair and stared at Vicki while wiping her mouth with a napkin. "You don't have much patience, do you?" she asked. Vicki was at the door about to open it when she turned to address the woman's question. "That's probably why your husband died a senseless death."

Vicki frowned, "What did you just say?" she asked while slowly approaching.

Calmly seated at the table, the woman asked, "Ain't you the least bit interested in knowing why, or who was responsible? Don't you wanna' find the piece of shit responsible?"

"Who the hell are you and what do you know about my man's death? And bitch, you betta'..."

"Betta' what?" the woman interrupted her in a calm, even tone. "Save your ass like I did the night you got your man murked?"

Vicki's left eye narrowed into a slit and her hands trembled with rage. "Bitch you don't know me!" It was at that moment when Vicki knew it was about to go down. The woman had hit a nerve that sent Vicki one minute from going postal. The woman who called herself, Camille had just accused her of being responsible for getting her husband killed.

52

No one have ever blamed her for such an atrocity. Not even her own mother-in-law.

"If you weren't so impatient. So full of yourself. Maybe he'd still be alive?"

Right then and there Vicki lost it and went straight for the fork. "BITCH! I'll kill You!" The woman was still seated when Vicki lunged forward. Without bothering to stand, the woman grabbed Vicki's wrist and twisted it in the opposite direction with very little effort. "AGH!" Vicki cried. A sharp pain shot up her arm, rendering her helpless. The woman continued twisting until Vicki dropped to her knees and released the fork.

Still seated, the woman sarcastically commented, "And they call you a threat? Bitch, please!"

Vicki sat helplessly on her knees in front of the woman and began to sob. The woman picked up the fork and sat it on the food-card before standing. She then helped Vicki to her feet and attentively guided her into the bedroom where Vicki curled up on her side on top of the bed and wept. The woman sat on the bed beside her.

"That's right, baby. Get it all out," she began soothing Vicki while gently rubbing her back in a circular motion. Vicki lips trembled as tears rolled down her face. "It's okay," the woman whisper. It was as if she had given Vicki permission to openly express her sorrow. Vicki could no longer hide her pain. She buried her face in the woman's lap and howled. "Shhh, shhh. I got you, baby. You don't have to feel alone anymore. I got you," the woman said while holding Vicki tight with both arms. "Yeah, that's right. Let it out. Get it all out of your system," she whispered in Vicki's ear while rocking her back and forth. "Everything is gonna' be fine. Lean on me, I got you. Camille will take care of you."

Still sobbing, Vicki looked up at her and tried to speak, "I... I...." but the words got caught in her throat.

"Shhh. You don't have to say anything. I know you sometime feel as if you're all alone. You're not, Vicki. You have me now," said Camille. She lightly kissed Vicki on the forehead, then cheek. "That's right, baby. Let it all out. Get it all out of your system."

Vicki cried until she couldn't cry anymore. While she silently laid in Camille's arms, she quickly drifted off to sleep. Camille waited until she was sure Vicki was asleep before removing Vicki's shoes and placing the covers over her. She then walked into the living area where she sat on the sofa to slip her knee-high boots back on before retrieving a large, black duffel-bag from the closet. She then slipped on her white leather jacket, pushed the food cart out into the hall before leaving the suite.

Flossing his borrowed rid, Asmar was cruising through the C.C.P. looking for Punchie when he spotted someone he thought might lead him to her. After parking, he walked around to the back of the building where a host of young hustlers had been hanging out. "What up, Az'?" asked a young hustler named, Wreak.

"What's good?" Asmar did not know Wreak by name, he just remembered seeing the youth chilling with Punchie a few times.

"Same ol' shit, son. First we lose 'Face, then Big Mike get pushed, and now Spivey. I don't know what's going on, son, but this shit is about to get crazy, you heard?"

"I heard. Yo', you see my punk-ass cousin, Punchie out here anywhere?" Asmar was well known and respected to all the young-bloods throughout P-town. And though he too was considered a young boy by the ol' heads, he was still considered a big brother to up and coming thugs.

"Naw, but it's early. She bound to pop up sooner or later. You want me to tell her you looking for her?"

"Naw, I'll see her." Asmar was about to leave when Punchie came out of the building with two young females that looked as if they were aspiring strippers. "Yo', bitch! I been looking for you! What type of shit you into? You trying to get me pushed?"

"Man, fuck you! You wasn't tryin' to find me when you had my loot."

"Bitch you know damn well I had you!"

"And how I'm suppose to know that? Y'all so full of shit. I ain't even trying to hear the shit y'all talking!"

"A'ight, bitch! I get your drift!" Asmar quickly cut her off. He then took her to the side and whispered, "Be careful what you say. Unless you want all these jokers out here to know we pushed your man on North Third."

"Jokers already talking. That's how I knew big Keys and them hit that joker up."

"Hold your vice down!" Asmar angrily cautioned. "Fuck you mean jokers already talking? Who the hell did you tell?"

"I ain't tell no body. Jokers talking 'bout some Jamaican dudes riding around with two other jokers asking questions about that joker, Spivey. I'm surprise you ain't heard. I heard all this from, Wreak. Said ol' boy was offering ten large for information, yo'."

"Yeah?"

"That's what Wreak said. It's all news to me, son."

"He tell you their names?"

"I ain't ask. Hell I wanna' know their name for. Bunck them jokers! They come my way talkin' that rowdy-rowdy shit. They gone get got. You feel me?"

"I feel you," Asmar smiled with pride at his little cousin who should have been born a boy.

"I got shit to do. Um' out, yo'" Punchie and her two companions walked off towards the down-town area.

Azmar waited until Punchie and her two companions were no longer in eye shot before pulling Wreak to the side and asking, "Jokers trying to give up ten grand around this mutha'?"

"Yeah. Some cut-up, dark skinned lame from the Islands. I think he said his name was, Khalif. He had some muscle with him. Two other hard looking Yardy boyz'. Them jokers had dread-locks that looked like tree trunks, yo'. Not that bitch shit you see these jokers wearing around here. Their shit was official, son. Real talk."

"What you tell 'em?"

"I ain't tell them shit, you feel me?"

"You sure, yo'?"

"I don't know shit, son. Hell yeah I'm sure."

"You know if they still around here?"

"They probably up on North Third. Spivey territory, you heard."

"A'ight. If you hear anything. Let me know, you heard?"

"I heard. Yo, Az', that your wheels you rolled up in here on?"

"It will be."

"That shit is official, son. Only other joker I seen pushing some shit like that was Big Mike."

"That's because it use to be his," Asmar wink before walking off.

57

# CHAPTER 5

Out of respect for the dead, SunRise deliberately waited before paying Vicki a visit. In his search for answers, the first person that came to mind was a barber shop owner in Harlem named, Reggy Ford. SunRise knew if the hit on Michael Henderson had anything to do with the raid on the stash-house in Regal Park, Reggy Ford knew about it. After all, it was Reggy who first brought the stash-house in Queens to SunRise's attention. SunRise wasn't sure if Johnathen Crain Junior, the man now tracking FOLD members was responsible for killing Michael Henderson and his men? He was, however, sure that Junior Crain was the man responsible for the murders of Melvin Vincent, his wife and her live-in nurse.

It was a bit early when SunRise called Tyrone from a pay-phone with instructions where to meet him. Forty minutes later Tyrone pulled up at a neighborhood store on North First street as instructed. One of the first things he did was look around for SunRise's car. Instead, he saw Michael Henderson's red Mustang Mach III parked in front of the small grocery store. SunRise's car had been parked right behind it.

Tyrone was about to enter the store when he spotted SunRise through the window heavily engaged in a conversation with someone Tyrone thought looked very familiar? It didn't take SunRise long before he noticed Tyrone trying to get his attention. Without taking his eyes from the man who had been 'bending his hear'. SunRise held up an index finger to indicate, one minute. Tyrone nodded in acknowledgment. He was about to wait in the car for SunRise, until he noticed two attractive females heading in his direction. "Morning ladies," he greeted them. The two females looked at him and smiled before walking into the store. Tyrone followed.

While he flirted with the two females inside the store. Every now and then he'd glance at SunRise to see if he had concluded his conversation with the man whose face looked very familiar. Shortly thereafter, SunRise signaled him to wait outside. Tyrone abruptly concluded his conversation with the two females then left the store to wait for the man-child in his car. Moments later, SunRise emerged from the store to joined him. "Isn't that Henderson's car parked in front of yours?" Tyrone curiously asked.

"Yeah."

"Who's driving it?"

"The brutha' you just saw me talking with in the store."

"So what's up? I tried calling Mr. Vincent all night, but no one answered. I haven't seen or heard from 'Sweet ether and I'm beginning to worry?" Before SunRise could answer, Tyrone asked another question. "Who was that guy you were just talking to? He looks familiar."

"Asmar West. Said he was a friend of Joey's."

"That's where I remember him, with Joey."

"Didn't you say Vicki told you a white woman let her into the house?"

"Yeah. Why?"

"Nothing about a white female was ever mentioned in the papers. According to Asmar, Michael Henderson's wife is hardly an assassin." SunRise thought for a moment and said, "I once heard Mike tried to have her murdered. Something about her infidelity?"

"I also heard he had her murdered, but I heard it was because she tried to leave him. Something about the work he was into. So she's back in town?" Tyrone asked.

SunRise noted an elevation in his voice. Almost as if he found the reappearance of the woman a pleasant surprise. "According to Asmar, everything Henderson owned was in her name."

"That was stupid. Unless he really loved her?"

"I need you to track her down. Maybe she can cast some light on the situation. Namely the woman who took her place in her husband's life. If you find her, keep an eye on her." SunRise took a quick peek at his watch. "Check around and find out if anyone knew if Henderson had a new girlfriend."

"What you gonna' do?"

"I'll be in touch," replied SunRise before exiting the car.

Forty-five minutes later, SunRise was in Harlem sitting in the back room of a neighborhood barbershop talking to the owner, Reggy Ford. Reggy was a part-time 'computer wiz' who fancied himself as a full-time comedian. A people's person, he was the proud owner of a barbershop left to him by his late father. As a child, Reggy use to hang out at his father's barbershop listening to the elder's talk amongst themselves. He admired his father and often dreamt of the day he was old enough to take up his father's trade. But Reggy's father wanted more for his only son. Often encouraging him to stay in school and think bigger. By age twelve, Reggy began taking interest in the young females in his neighborhood, but they weren't interested in him. Half blind in his right eye, he wore glasses that were anything but flattering. The left lens in his glasses was normal while the right lens was so think, it magnified the appearance of his right eye. Making him the bud of everyone's joke. But as an aspiring comedian, Reggy knew how to take a joke. As a matter of fact; he was better at telling them. And later became known for his sharp and witty come-backs that were so funny, he often had the crowd rolling with laughter.

After Reggy's father passed, be kept the barbershop open mostly to give the elders a place to sit and talk as they often have when he was a child.

SunRise, however, was not there to congregate with the old-heads. He was there for information, which was Reggy's forte. The way Reggy saw it, everyone had a secret to hide. Find their secret and you become the most powerful person in their lives. SunRise needed all the information on a certain Brooklyn Lieutenant by the name of, Ralph Sheets.

"Gim' me twenty-four hours and I'll have everything you need. Including how many teeth in his mouth are real."

"You have one hour," SunRise said before producing the copy of the disk.

"Is that the same disk you found at the house in Queens? The one you had me open for you a few weeks ago?" Reggy immediately asked.

"Yeah," said SunRise while handing Reggy the disk. "I need you to take another look at it in case you missed something.

Reggy looked at SunRise strangely and said, "So all that other shit we found on it wasn't enough?" It was a rhetorical question which was why SunRise never bothered to answer. "I'll see what I can do," said Reggy before changing the subject. "The Dominicans who rented that house in Queens were all found murdered two days after making bail. Word is, the shipment came straight from Columbia. Prepaid by the Dominicans in the Republic. Um' guessing Hector Figueroa had it shipped to his nephew, Teflon. Them cats from Washington Heights got shit on lock. Shit, everybody was under the impression your boy Michael Henderson had a direct pope-line. Word on the street was he was suppose be the next king of the tri-state area? WRONG JEOPARDY ANSWER!" Reggy shouted with a crazy laugh. "You don't get pushed for losing your own shipment. But for loosing another joker's shit? You get got."

"What about the disk?" SunRise quickly asked.

"What about it?"

"Are they looking for it?"

"Who?"

"The Dominicans."

"I haven't heard anything. Gim'me  a few hours to see what I can come up with ?"

"I'll be back in one hour. Have something I can use, Reggy."

Reggy tapped his right fist over his left breast twice while assuring SunRise if there was anything to find on the disk, he would find it.

With an hour to kill. SunRise had another stop to make while he was in the neighborhood. He had never been to Mama's Place, but heard a lot of good things about it. Things such as;  how it had managed to succeed where other small businesses in the area had went under.

Mama's Place was more than just a small family business. It was a landmark. A piece of black history that managed to survive unfavorable  odds. SunRise remembered a New York journalist who did a partial story on the small, family owned restaurant. Since, folks came from all over to support and taste some of Mama's specialties. After which a host of other problems began to arise.

First, there were the developers trying to buy the small family owned business out. When that didn't work, stooges were hired to discredit their reputation in an effort to discourage patrons from patronizing the small family business with hopes of forcing them to sell. But that didn't work either. Of course the small family owned restaurant lost a lot of business. Still, they were tough. Use to withstanding considerable amounts of hardship. SunRise himself remembered hearing some nasty things said about, 'MAMA'S PLACE'. Things that were neither here nor there. He knew the game, a bunch of greedy business-men who did the math and realized the money that could be made in the right location. What those greedy businessmen fail to take into account was, MAMA'S PLACE had been in business for a lot of years and in that time, never had any complaints. That is, until recently. This, however, did not stop loyal customers from patronizing the family greasy-spoon.

The moment SunRise walked into the restaurant, he was warmly greeted by a pleasant old woman who immediately asked, "Would you like a table, sweetie?"

"Yes, I would. Thank you."

After he was seated, the old woman gave him a menu. "I'll give you a moment to look it over," she said before leaving to wait on another customer.

SunRise looked over the menu which consisted of all sorts of southern, home-style specialties such as; southern fried chicken, greens, candy-yams, dumplings, fried shrimp, potato- salad, and northern and southern style cornbread amongst a host of other tasty treats. Still, it was much too early for such a heavy meal and he have not had breakfast yet.

A few minutes later, the old woman returned. "Have you decided yet, sweetie?"

"As a matter of fact, I have. I'll try the southern-style breakfast."

"You want coffee, or juice with that?"

"A black coffee and large glass of freshly squeezed orange juice would be nice. Thank you."

As SunRise waited for his meal, he spotted two old-timers at another table enjoy their meal. The moment they noticed him looking their way, one of them smiled and waved. SunRise returned the gesture with a simple nod.

After the woman brought his meal, he placed a napkin over his lap and was about to eat when one of the old-timers asked him to join them. Casually gathering up his meal, he joined the two elders at their table.

"Good-morning, gentlemen," SunRise greeted the two men.

"How's it going?" one of them replied between bits.

"Not too good, I'm afraid," SunRise said. "I was hoping to speak with one of the workers here about a friend of mine. By the way, I'm SunRise." SunRise extended his hand to the first old-timer.

"Oh, hell no!" said the first old-timer while ignoring SunRise's extended hand." I don't do no hand shakin' while eatin'. No sir," he said while stuffing a fork of hash-browns in his mouth. "No offense, but that shit ain't sanitary. Don't know where you young folk hands been."

SunRise laughed a little before replying, "No offense taken, Sir. And actually, you're right. It isn't sanitary and I apologize."

"Oh don't mind him," said the second old-timer while placing his fork on his plate to extend his hand. "Um' Bomen, but friends call me Bo. This here is Nathan," he said, referring to his friend.

"No, no." SunRise held up both hands. "Your friend, Nathan here is right, Bo." SunRise paused briefly, "Oh, I'm sorry. May I call you, Bo?"

"We friends, ain't we?"

SunRise smiled, "I would like to think so."

"Then it's settled. Call me, Bo," he insisted before continuing while putting his extended hand down. "You said you looking to speak to one of the workers?" asked Bo.

"If you lookin' for work, or somethin'. I don't think they gon' hire you," said Nathan.

"Not unless you family?" Bo quickly interject.

"Nothing like that, sir."

"SIR! Damn, Bo. He called you, sir."

Bo looked at his friend, Nathan and proudly pointed out, "That's what you call respect." He then looked at SunRise and asked, "Where you from, Sunshine? 'Cause you damn sure ain't from around here."

"SUNSHINE!" shouted, Nathan. "Why you call that boy, Sunshine? His name ain't no damn, Sunshine! That'sa girl's name. Damn Sunshine! That boy jump on yo' ass, don't look for no help from me?"

Bo looked at his friend, Nathan and said, "Well that's his name." He then looked at SunRise and asked, "Ain't that your name, son?"

"Actually it's SunRise."

Bo frowned confused. "Say what?"

"My name. It's SunRise. And no, I'm not from around here. I understand a friend of mine had dinner here a few days ago. I also heard she was arrested right outside afterwards. I was told, before they took..."

"You say, she?" Nathan interrupted.

"Yes. The person I'm referring to was a female. Tall, beautiful, dark-skinned with long, thick dread-locks. You remember seeing her?"

"Yeah, I remember her, but she was hardly a beauty queen," said Nathan while looking at his friend, Bo. "You remember, Bo. That girl they arrested. Happen right here 'cross the street. Had all kinda' cops out here."

"I remember," Bo began. " FBI came and got her. Don't know where they took her, but they must of let her go 'cause not too long afterwards, she show up again. Saw her getting out of a car right there," he stood, walked over to the window to pointed up the street.

68

"You noticed which way she went?" SunRise quickly asked.

"Cross the street to her car. I tried to get her attention to let her know some of them FBI boys was sitting in their car watching her, but she didn't see me. Musta' saw them, though. She got in her car and tore outta' here like it was no tomorrow."

"Did they go after her?"

"Hell yeah they went after her. What I couldn't understand was why they let her go just to arrest her again?"

SunRise thought about it and remembered what he had learned from TooSweet and Sunny Black. He picture the events of the two old-timer's story in his mind, and came up with a single conclusion.

After returning to the barber-shop an hour later, Reggy immediately asked, "What took you, man? I've been waiting for twenty minutes."

"I said one hour. It's been an hour. No more, no less."

Reggy frowned and scratched his head. "Oh," then burst out laughing. When he noticed SunRise was hardly in the mood to be amused. He cleared his throat and led SunRise to his office in back.

Inside his office, he handed SunRise a hard copy of a file on Lieutenant Sheets' background. As SunRise carefully thumbed through the folder. He saw something he found interesting and looked up at Reggy. Reggy smiled. "I told you I got you, 'Rise. Check out pages five, six and seven," he urged while snickering.

SunRise quickly flipped to the suggested pages. "So that's what it was all about, huh. The old man wants to become a politician?"

Reggy busted out into a fit of laughter. "You want me to put a couple of females on him?" he asked, still snickering.

SunRise thought about it, but declined. "More power to him. If the man wants to get into politics, god bless him. My only concern was whether or not he was involved with the people whose name were found on the disk. Turns out, he's just what he appears to be, a cop. Now that that's over, tell me you found something I don't know on the disk?" SunRise changed the subject.

Reggy smiled while handing SunRise the disk. "You were right, 'Rise. The shit I found on this disk reads like a journal. You couldn't paid me to believe the Dominicans at the house in Queens created this disk for the people they worked for?" Reggy stopped what he was doing to look at SunRise. "Check this shit out," he said while clicking on a second lower-case I from the word committee. He then expanded it until three names that were hidden within the dot of the lowercase I, appeared. Johnathen Crain, Napoleon Webb and Mona Leigh.

"We know Johnathen Crain, but who are the other two and what does it means?"

"It means I found what you were looking for. Which was what you're paying me for. I can't tell you what it means exactly. That's something you gonna' have to figure out on your own."

"The night you broke the code when I brought you the disk a few weeks ago. What was the pass-word you used to get in?"

Reggy laughed. "A stipper's name."

"What's the name?" he asked again with hopes of recognizing it.

Reggy laughed some  more and said, "Mystique. Ring any bells for you?" he casually asked with a knowing smile.

"No," SunRise said disappointingly. "You have any thoughts on it?"

"Not really. But I'll say this, whoever that password belonged to, can't spell worth a damn," he laughed. "They spelled, mystique  m-s-t-i-q-u-e." He bust out with a crazy laugh that almost  put a smile on SunRise's face. Once he realized he was dealing with a rough crowd, he cleared his throat and said, "I just thought you should know. Again, that's what you pay me for." He laughed that crazy laugh of his again. Only this time SunRise smiled, but not because he shared in Reggy's humor. It was because Reggy was one of the best computer technicians on this side of the coast and SunRise knew he wasn't telling him everything.

"What's this?" SunRise asked.

"What's what?"

"This." SunRise pointed out the list of numbers that didn't seem to make sense.

"Oh, that. I suspect account numbers."

"As in, bank account numbers?"

"More than likely. I suspect the account are off shore. Which was why I took the liberty to start searching for off shore bank names, and hidden locations within the journal. I found one bank, two different account."

"Which would explain the two set of numbers." SunRise looked at Reggy with annoyance.

"What?" Reggy asked.

"When were you planning on telling me all this?"

"When you asked," Reggy said with that crazy laugh of his. "Um' just playing, 'Rise," he continued while composing himself. "Whoever made the journal must have been ...'"

"Accumulating information. Why, is the pivotal question?" SunRise finished Reggy's sentence for him. The thing about Reggy, he was a terrible liar.

"So far," Reggy continued. "I came up with a bank in the Caymans. I just need more time to find the pass-word?" he paused with hopes of SunRise granting him more time to work with the disk, but when SunRise didn't answer, he changed the subject. "More than likely, both of those accounts are cloaked."

"If they weren't accumulating the information for the people they worked for. Who do you suppose they were compiling it for?" asked SunRise.

Reggy paused for a moment before verbalizing his thoughts. "What about the feds? To get that kind of personal information, they had to use some type of spy-ware programs. Like a Trojan horses, cookies, or data miners. They're placed on your hard drive. Jokers be knowing everything you do on your computer. Even the web-sites you've visited."

"A what?"

A Trojan horse. The government came up with it. Now-a-days, the FBI searches e-mails looking for extremist by screening for key words. They don't even need a court order anymore. Shit, now-days, a virus protection program wouldn't even shield you from Uncle-Sam."

"Why?"

"Mainly because they forced all the companies that manufacture security programs to agreed not to install blocking programs in their anti-virus programs and fire-walls. In other words, the government can and may read anything you send on the 'net."

"You said a Trojan horse is placed on the back of the hard drive?"

"You can also insert them from a 'site or through software you load. I know jokers who can attach them to an E-mail and send it to you. As soon as you open the E-mail, they're in. Haven't you ever wondered how companies get your information to send you shit and actually know your first name? That's that Spy-ware shit. The moment you log on to their 'site, they're in.

"How would you know?"

"It slows your computer down. While it's collecting data about you, it's eating up a lot of memory. Look, 'Rise," Reggy quickly changed the subject. "with your permission. I'd like a little more time to work on it. If I can find the pass-word to the accounts. I can have the money transferred into your account. All I need is your bank's routing number, your account number, social security number and pass-ward. Hit a few keys and BAM! You the richest cat in the 'hood. Of course I'll need thirty percent of the combined take?" Reggy thought he'd give it a shot. When SunRise looked at him with a serious stare, he burst out laughing. "Just joking with you, 'Rise. Man... you shoulda' seen your face," he said while still laughing.

"We done, Reggy?" SunRise immediately interrupted him."

"Yeah... unless you want me to make that transaction happen?" SunRise shot him a hard look. "Just kidding, 'Rise. You gotta' learn to lightin' up, yo'. Relax a lil', damn! You all stiff in shit."

"Do I look like I have the time to be entertained?" Once Reggy realized how serious SunRise was being, he took a different approach. It was the only approach SunRise could appreciated.

"If the IRS get a hold of this disk. Every name on it is going to jail." Reggy paused while studying SunRise carefully before suggesting, "You might wanna' throw a little bonus my way. I did a thorough search to access this information. Umma' beast when it comes to this shit. Oh yeah, even thought you never ask? I also have the pass-word to both accounts," he boosted before handing SunRise the hard copy of what he had found.

"It wouldn't happen to be the word, committee, would it?" SunRise asked while scanning through the hard-copy Reggy just handed him.

"Reggy looked at him strangely and asked, "How the hell could you know that?"

"As always, you did good, Reggy." He then handed Reggy the five bill as promised.

"You need me to work on a hit on those three names we just found?" Reggy asked.

"Naw. I think I can handle it," said SunRise before adding, "I'll be in touch, Reggy." He then left without bothering to wait for a reply.

Reggy shouted after him, "WHAT! NO BONUS?"

Without stopping or answering, SunRise just glanced over his shoulder at Reggy with a vague smile while exiting the shop. Reggy shouted, "Can't blame a brutha' for trying!" then busted out laughing.

It was almost noon when SunRise arrived at Vicki's mother- in-law's apartment. He didn't really expect her to be there, but he had to start somewhere. With almost all of the pieces to the puzzle, he could no longer put off seeing her.

At the door, SunRise was confronted by a middle aged woman who turned out to be the landlady. Regretfully, she had informed him that the reverend Matty Dixson had passed away in her sleep and was found by her daughter-in-law Sunday morning.

"I couldn't be more sorry to hear that," SunRise immediately expressed his condolence before continuing. "Do you by any chance know where I might be able to locate the reverend's daughter-in-law?"

"Well... she took the reverend's passing kinda' hard. We found her curled up in bed with the reverend, crying. Poor child. They had to pry her from the reverend's body. I was there when it happened. It's a shame. Buried her husband one day and her mother-in-law passes the next. Lord Jesus."

"Do you know where I might be able to find her?" he asked again.

The woman thought for a moment. "Well... deacon Willie came by earlier this morning to pick up some fresh clothing for her. Said he was gonna' pick her up from the hospital. That had to be four hours ago. They shoulda' been back by now? Some young woman came by yesterday looking for her?"

"You said something about someone picking her up from the hospital?"

The landlady looked at SunRise strangely. "Yeah, baby. Wasn't you listening? When they tried to remove the reverend's body, she lost it. Went completely crazy. They had to give her something to calm her down. Said they were gonna' hold her overnight for observation."

"You said Deacon Willie went to pick her up? Is he a deacon, or something?"

"He's one of the deacon's at the church. He was the one who had me check when the reverend never showed up for special services yesterday morning. I knew something wasn't right 'cause she never missed a service. When he told me he tried calling, but no one answered? I started to worry. I knew someone was home. Heard crying in there all morning. I just thought the girl was grieving. You know, the lost of her husband and all. When the deacon came by and said Matty never showed up for services? Went and got my spear. You know, just to make sure everything was all right? I can't remember Matty ever missing a services. I seen her walk to church in a storm one morning last year."

"Of course. Can you tell me where I can find the deacon?" SunRise politely asked.

"About two houses down."

"Thank you for your time. And again, I am truly sorry to hear about Reverend Dixson. I didn't know her personally, but from what I hear? She will be missed."

"Ain't that the truth. Ain't gonna' be the same around here without her. You going to the funeral?" asked the woman.

"If I don't make it? I will send flowers along with my condolence."

"All right, baby. You take care now."

"You too, Ma'am." SunRise was about to turn to leave, but stopped to ask the woman another question. "Oh, yeah. You said, some female came over looking for Vicki yesterday?"

"Yeah. Some young woman. I told her Vicki was in the hospital for observation."

"Did she leave a name?"

"No name. No."

"Can you tell me how she looked?"

The woman thought for a moment. "Well, she was white, young, dressed casual, but nice. Probably in her early twenties. I don't remember what color her hair was, but I do remember it being short. Oh yeah, she wore some big, black, shiny shades. They looked expensive? She a friend of yours?"

"I certainly hope she's not foe. Thanks again, Ma'am."

"Anytime, baby."

SunRise followed the landlady's direction and walked a few houses down. The only house left was another old apartment building almost identical to the one he had just left. As he approached, an elderly man carrying a large, brown, paper bag came up behind him and entered the building. "'Cuse me, sir?" He followed the old man into the building. "Came you please tell me if a deacon Willie stays at this residence?"

"Well now, that depends on whose asking, young man," said the elder.

"My name is, SunRise,"

"SunRise! Well I'll be. What kinda' name is that for a fine young man such as yourself? Now I know your parents ain't give you no name like, SunRise."

"No... they didn't, sir. Anyway, I was told I could find Deacon Willie at this address by a woman who lives a few houses up. I'm trying to locate Vicki Lane, daughter-in-law to the late Reverend Dixson."

He eyed SunRise with a curious suspicion. "I see," he said. "You a friend of hers?"

"I'd like to think so."

"Well I can't help you, young man."

"Perhaps you could direct me to Deacon Willie. I understand he was suppose to pick her up at the hospital this morning?"

"I'm deacon Willie, son. Vicki left the hospital before I got there. See..." he held up the brown paper bag. "... I still have the change of clothing I was suppose to bring her. One of the nurses said she saw Vicki talking to some girl outside the hospital after she was released this morning." He paused in thought before continuing. "Come to think of it, Stella said a girl came at the house yesterday looking for Vicki. Couldn't have been the same girl, though. Nurse said the girl she saw taking with Vicki was Latino. Stella told me the girl who came by the house yesterday was a white girl."

"Did the nurse give you a description of the woman?"

"You mean other than being Latino?" he smiled and continued. "About Vicki's age, not as tall, medium built, short, straight black hair. The nurse said they talked for a while, then left in the woman's car."

"Did Vicki know you were coming to pick her up?"

"No. She didn't know."

"Did the nurse say what kind of car the woman was driving?"

"Yes she did. I remember, 'cause she kept telling me how hard she was trying to get her husband to buy her one for Christmas. It was a... let me see," he held his head up to the sky and closed his eyes trying to recall what the nurse said. "GOT IT!" he shouted while snapping his finger. "It was a white 1993 Nissan."

"Thank you, sir." SunRise said before turning to leave. "Yeah, yeah, no problem, son. I just hope she's all right," the elderly man concluded.

SunRise turned without stopping and said, "As do I, sir."

# CHAPTER 6

Later that night, Tyrone found himself sitting on a stool in a downtown pool-hall talking to a thirty-eight year old woman named Renee Gantley. As a single mother of a teenage son, she was well known and liked around town. As a pool shark, she never hid the fact that she was a hustler. She didn't have to. After all, she was a women who often counted on the male ego to not only shoot her a game, but up the stake as well. No man who spent the better portion of his day hanging out in a pool-hall wanted to believe they could ever be beaten by a female. Which was the only edge she needed.

Renee' was an attractive woman who, for whatever reason, never gave her beauty the credit it deserved. And because she never wore make-up to enhance what she already had. Her flawless golden-brown skin-tone complimented her Asian shaped, dark brown eyes. Which, by the way, was one of her most attractive features. Unfortunately, Renee often hid them behind a pair of plain eye-glasses she thought gave her face character. The truth was, her thick black perfectly arched brows and naturally long, thick lashes gave her face character.

Of average height, Renee wore long, thick dread-locks she took very good care of. Still, most men never looked at her long enough to find her attractive. Mostly because she was a black woman whose weight border-lined anorexia. Still, she was the type of person who could talk to anyone, and anyone could talk to her. Tyrone Sharp not only found her approachable, but also the perfect source for information.

"You heard about your boy, Michael Henderson?" Tyrone threw the name out there. The last thing he wanted to do was come straight out and ask about Henderson's wife.

"My boy! Shit! He wasn't no boy of mine. I would never fuck with some dude who's been south of the border, you know what um' sayin'?" she laughed a little.

"I feel you. Which reminds me, I saw Asmar driving Henderson's car. What's up with that?"

"Asmar West?"

"Yeah, I guess that's his name."

"With his lil' nasty ass. Always thinking with his dick. As soon as that bitch shows up in town, he was on her. Gotta' hand it to him, though. Lil' nasty ass got the gift of gab. He's just gabbing at the wrong bitch."

"Who you talking about?"

"Mike's wife. That bitch playing his dumb ass just like she played Mike's stupid ass.

"You sure we talking about the same woman?"

"Yeah. That trifling-ass bitch."

"You said she played Mike? Played him, how?"

Renee' looked at Tyrone strangely. "You must be the only joker who don't know?"

"Don't know what?"

"Before that fool got with that pale-ass-bitch. He was doing all right copping three, or four kilos at a time. At least then, he didn't owe anyone. That bitch talked his stupid ass into copping weight on consignment."

"How they meet?"

"Who the fuck knows. I heard his connect introduced them."

"I heard she was fucking around on Mike?"

"That bitch will fuck anyone she can get her hands on," she said with a laugh.

"What's so funny?"

"Mike. Running around town like he had a choice bitch. Stupid muthafucka'. Now that bitch gets everything he had. Which can't be much."

"Mike had to have a lil' something stashed away? Or am I missing something?"

"Michael Henderson didn't have shit, but that car and probably some cash. I heard the house was even a lease. I guess she'll be using Asmar dumb ass next. I saw his little ass driving someone else's car like he-the-shit." She leaned towards Tyrone's ear and whispered in confidence, "I'll bet anything that bitch set Mike's stupid ass up from the rip. Personally, I think she's up to something." She paused a moment in thought. Then said with a proud smile, "Gotta' hand it to her, though. The bitch is gansta'."

"Damn, baby. Do I detect a hint of jealousy?"

"Hell yeah um' jealous," she said jokingly with a little laugh. "I ain't gonna' front, shit. Bitch like me can't find shit."

"That's because you've been looking in all the wrong places."

She looked at him peculiar. "So what you saying?"

"I'm saying there's a lot of bruthas' out here who would love to get with a fine sista' like you, Renee'."

"Yeah, right!"

"I'm serious!" Tyrone said before putting his point through the test. "You see that brutha' over there?" he directed her attention a few tables down.

"Where? Nigga' you full of shit!"

"Two tables down. You can't miss him."

Without being too obvious, Renee took her time and carefully scanned the entire room. Observing each guy individually. When she got to the second table down. She didn't notice anything out of the ordinary about the two guys using the table. Just as she was about to move on, she notice one of the guys at that table checking her out. He was a handsome tall light-brown skinned guy with golden blond dread-locks. "All I see are a bounce of jokers trying to get their sorry ass pool game up."

"Look again, sista'."

"You talking about that fine-ass nigga' with the blond dreads?" she asked with hopes Tyrone confirmed her suspicions.

"That's exactly who I'm talking about."

She blushed. "Not my type," she lied.

"That's what's wrong with you, baby-girl. You too picky."

"Picky! Nigga, please!"

"The brutha' has been shooting me bricks every since I pulled up a seat next to you. But knowing you, you'll find some excuse not to give him the time of day. I know how you women think. You have a habit of shutting jokers down even before they get started."

"That's because most of these fools just coming home from jail looking for a bitch like me to take care of 'em. Renee ain't the one."

"That's your first problem. Your second problem is your mouth. If you present yourself like you're from the streets. Bruthas' gonna' treat you like you're from the streets. Stop swearing so much. It's not attractive at all. Especially coming from someone as sweet as you."

"Yeah, right. These jokers can talk shit, but us bitches ain't suppose to? Ain't that some shit!"

"I'm just saying...." The minute Tyrone realized he was getting nowhere, he changed the subject. "You wouldn't happen to know who Mike's connect was, would you?" Tyrone thought he'd give it a shot.

"His name? No. I just heard that's how he met his wife. Some lame from his camp mentioned it. I think he was trying to get with me, but I don't do hustlers. Those fools got a short shelf-life, you know what I'm saying?" she exaggerated her laugh while glancing at the men shooting pool two tables down.

"I feel you. Back to your girl, Henderson's wife."

"My girl? Shit! Bitch like that could never roll with a bitch like me."

"I heard Mike found another piece? Another white woman with blond hair. You know who she is, or where I can find her?"

"Hell no! Why the hell would I know that?"

"What about his connect? His boy ever mention who his connect was?"

She looked at him with annoyance and shouted, "Nigga' didn't you just ask me that!"

"Yeah, yeah. You righ'. My bad. What about a man named, Johnathen Crain Junior?"

"What about him?"

"Did Mike's boy ever mention that name before?"

She looked at Tyrone peculiar and leaned back in her chair and stared at him. "Now why the fuck would I remember some shit like that? You askin' a lot of questions?"

"Just making conversation, that's all. They ever talk about Mike's lawyer?"

She looked at him with the same annoyance and shouted, "I told you, nigga'! I don't know! In fact, why don't you go ask that bitch, Catherine. Hell, she's staying right up the street at the, Alexander."

"She staying at the, Alexander?"

"Yeah, fool! What? You hard of hearing all of a sudden?"

Tyrone smiled. "Okay, baby-girl. Thanks," he said while standing to leave. "Just remember what I said about your mouth."

"Baby. Renee' too old to change." she replied. He shook his head, kissed her on the cheek and left.

Just around the corner from the hotel in question. Tyrone left his car parked on Market street and walked the rest of the way. He thought about seeing her again and tried to picture her face, but couldn't. He only saw her once or twice in the past, and remembered feeling guilty about being so attracted to a white woman. He tried, but for some reason, he couldn't remember what he found so attractive about her?

Inside the hotel's lobby, several people came and went as if they were in a hurry. Tyrone scanned the area with hopes of spotting Catherine in the crowded lobby, but didn't recognize anyone. Reluctantly he approached the front desk. There were two desk-clerks working. A young white male and an elderly white woman. Both were busy at the time with guest checking in, or checking out. After a few minutes of waiting, the young male looked at him and asked, "Yes, Sir. May I help you?"

Tyrone leaned on the desk and tried to speak privately, but the woman immediately came over and asked the very same question the young male had just asked.

"I'm being taken care of, Ma'am, thank you," he quickly dismissed her. Without so much as a courtesy smile she could at the very least, fake. She rolled he eyes at him before reluctantly tending to another guest.

"What, she don't trust you to do your job?" he asked the young man, trying to establish some type of rapport.

The young clerk smiled politely and replied, "I think she's just making sure everyone is properly taken care of, Sir. This is my third day on the job. I'm sure she was just making certain there were no problems. How, may I help you?"

"I'm here to see a Mrs. Henderson. Mrs. Catherine Henderson. What room is she staying in?"

The young clerk immediately scanned through the records and spotted her name. "Is she expecting you, sir?"

"No, I don't believe she is."

"I'm sorry, sir. I can't give out any information about our guest. However, I will be happy to inform her that someone is here to see her if you'll just give me your name," he paused before continuing. "It's the only way I can give you her room number. Providing she agrees to see you. You understand."

"Of course," replied Tyrone. He knew Catherine agreeing to see him was a long shot. After all, she didn't know him at all. He also knew it was a waste of time, but at least he could tell SunRise he tried. "Tyrone Sharp. If it's not too much trouble, can you please tell her it's important that I speak with her?"

The clerk smiled, "No trouble at all, sir," he said while placing the receiver to his ear. Tyrone anxiously waited as the clerk spoke into the receiver. "Yes, this is the front desk. I have a..." he looked at Tyrone to repeat his name.

"Tyrone Sharp."

"Tyrone Sharp here at the desk. He says it's important that he speaks with you. Yes, ma'am. Will do." As the clerk hung up, Tyrone waited for the clerk to give him her answer. "She'll be right down, sir." Tyrone smiled and thanked the clerk before taking a seat in the lobby.

About five minutes later, he spotted two women getting off of the elevator. Tyrone recognized her immediately. Dressed in a conservative light-gray pant suit and white cotton blouse. She was on her way over to the desk when he stood and called out to her.

"Mrs. Henderson?"

She stopped, turned and looked at him as if she somehow knew who he was. As she approached, he cleared his throat and extended his hand. "Tyrone Sharp?" she asked while shaking his hand. There was a vague smile on her face. He wanted to ask her have they met before, but decided against it. She was stunning and not what he had expected at all. He had remembered seeing her in the past from a distance. But had been unable to remember what it was he found so attractive about her? Seeing her up close now, he finally remembered. He wished he could say it was her ass, tits, legs, or hips, but it wasn't as simple as that. Catherine Henderson had an air about her Tyrone found hard to resist.

Personally, he was not into white women. Although he had to admit, she was fine. Her yellowish blond hair was long and lavishly styled that gave her a sophisticated look. He also couldn't help noticing her eyes. She had the most captivating eyes he had ever seen. They were a light bluish-gray in color and by far, her best feature. He had guessed her to be in her mid thirties. Tall for a woman and a little thin for his taste, but shapely.

"Yes," he found himself a loss for words.

"What's this all about?" she asked, trying to get straight to the point as they both sat.

For a lack of anything else to say, he simply replied, "Your late husband."

"What about him?"

"After you left him, he found comfort in another woman. Someone, I was told who bears a striking resemblance to you?"

She smiled. He didn't think it was because she was flattered. He thought it was because she knew her late husband all too well. "Typical," she said, waiting for Tyrone to continue.

"Do you happen to know who the woman was, or where I can find her?"

"No. Why?"

"I think she might be responsible for the murder of your husband," he said in no uncertain terms. He had hoped to elicit some type of reaction, but the woman was unmoved by his theory. "In fact," he went on to say. "I think she murdered everyone in the house. Which makes her a professional. Do you know why anyone would have paid to have your husband murdered?"

"Are you a cop?" her eyes narrowed into slits as she gazed at him suspiciously. "Because I've already been questioned by the police. The same thing I told them, I will now tell you. I don't know anything about my late husband's affairs."

Tyrone's brows rose. "A cop! Hell no."

"Then who are you and why the hell are you asking me all these questions like I'm suppose to know something about my dead husband's affairs? Mister, I don't know nothing and if I did? What makes you think I'd tell you anything?" She stood and was about to walk away when Tyrone stopped her.

"Mrs. Henderson, wait!" He pleaded for more of her time. She stopped, turned and stared at him as if waiting to hear what else he had to say. There was something very sexual about her. Something that really turned him on. "I apologize if I wasn't as open with you as I should have been. Please," he motioned with a wave of his hand for her to sit. Once they were both seated again, he continued. "I work for an organization known as, FOLD. An anti drug organization who strongly believe in what we do. Our primary goal is to help rid the community of the distribution, sale and use of illegal drugs."

She smiled apathetically and replied, "Good luck."

He could have sworn she glanced at his crotch and felt himself getting excited. "Look, whoever murdered your husband, also murdered three of his men and two other hired assassins. That's six bodies, five of which were killers themselves and two of them were professionals. I'm here because you could be in danger." He had no idea what he had just said, but was hoping it all made sense to her.

She smiled, "Really. And why would anyone want to harm me. I left Mike long before...." she was about to say something, but decided against it. He could see she was beginning to worry. He also noticed she could no longer look him in the eye, or stop fidgeting with her hands.

"Long before what?" he asked, searching her face for the slightest bit of deception. "Mrs. Henderson, please. These people ain't playing. I think you know that."

Somewhat hesitant, she finally said, "... before he became involved with those people."

"What people?" he asked with hopes of a more informative answer.

Instead, she became agitated by the question. "Look. I really didn't know anything about Michael's business. I just knew I couldn't live that life-style, so I lift.

"And he just let you leave?"

She smiled again and said, "I would like to say the split was mutual, but nothing is ever that simple. Now if you'll excuse me. I have some things I have to do." She stood.

Tyrone stood with her. "Of course, and thank you for your time."

"Sorry I couldn't be of more help," she replied before walking away. As she strolled off to the elevator, Tyrone watched. Hoping she would give him a 'second take', but it didn't happen. Once again, he wasn't sure, but he could have sworn she glanced at his crotch before leaving.

As he casually walked towards the exit, he glanced over his shoulder to catch one last glimpse of her. She was just about to board the elevator when two men who had also been sitting in the lobby, approached her. At first Tyrone didn't think anything of it. That is, until he saw her pointing at him. His first thoughts were, cops. Apparently they had been watching the entire time. The last thing he wanted was to hang around to see what their interest could possibly be in him.

The moment he hit the streets, he quickly walked around the corner to his car and got in. While sitting behind the wheel, he saw the two men suddenly appear at the corner and began looking around. Suspecting they were looking for him, he ducked while wondering  why the sudden interest in him?

Once they had assumed he was gone, they got into a brand new white, 1994 Jeep Cherokee and just sat there. A few minute later. Asmar West, the young man he had seen talking to SunRise at the stores earlier, walked up to the Cherokee and began speaking to the two men. Tyrone watched while both men nodded in acknowledgment before finally pulling off. He wanted to have a long talk with Asmar. Mainly for blowing smoke up SunRise's ass.  But other matters that were far more important command his immediate attention.

Twenty-five minutes later, Tyrone's pursuit of the Cherokee lead him to Houston Street in lower Manhattan. While the jeep pulled onto the lot of a large, plush apartment building, he kept driving to avoid arising suspicion.

He drove around the block once before parking across the street from the building. There were at least fifteen units and he had no way of knowing which apartment the men occupied. Nor did he have any intentions of staking the building out all night. He was tired and in desperate need of sleep. But first, he wanted to make sure he had the exact address of the apartment building before leaving.

Unsure of his next move, he reached for his car-phone and proceeded to call SunRise. While waiting for SunRise to pick up. He never noticed the two men approaching the car until someone abruptly snatched the car door open. When he turned to see what was going on. He felt a painful blow to his jaw. Darkness ensued.

# NEMESIS III

# CHAPTER 7

Tyrone woke-up on the floor of a dimly lit room. A little confused as to where he was, or how he had gotten there? The first persons he saw was one of the two suits from the white Cherokee jeep. He shook his head trying to clear away the confusion, then noticed the second man from the jeep standing behind the first man. The moment Tyrone tried to stand, one of the suits, a stocky built man of medium height with huge muscular arms kicked him in the face. Darkness soon followed.

Awaken by an annoying slap to his face, Tyrone was in excruciating pain. Instinctively, he grabbed the left side of his jaw and tasted blood in his mouth. His jaw felt like it had been broken, but because he was able to rotate it, he knew it wasn't.

"Get up, pretty-boy. Someone wants to have a word with you," one of the men said.

"Yo, man. What's going on?" he asked while standing. Neither of the men answered. He looked around with hopes of seeing Catherine, but she was nowhere in sight. "Can I at least know who wanna' talk to me?"

The stocky built man who appeared to have been calling the shots between the two, simply replied, "You can." Tyrone waited for the man to answer his question, but no answer had been forth coming.

"Well? Who the fuck is it?" he all but yelled out of frustration. The stocky built man glanced at his associate, who walked up to Tyrone and smacked him with his gun across the left side of the face. Tyrone heard bells and saw stars long before the pain registered to his brain. He heard the stocky built man chuckle. Then felt himself being lifted by his arm. It was the stocky built man standing him up on his feet. Still somewhat dazed, Tyrone watched as the man with the imposing arms placed his weapon under his left arm in a shoulder holster. He then hit Tyrone with an upper-cut to the gut. Tyrone dropped to his knees and folded like a bad poker hand.

"Does that answer your question, or do you have something else you wanna' ask?" Still on his knees, Tyrone was wheezing for air. "I didn't think so," said the man while grabbing Tyrone by the arm again and dragging him to a nearby chair where he was forced to sit. He was then blindfolded with a cotton cloth that did not completely blind him, just obscured his vision. A few moments later, he heard the door open, then close. Unable to see two feet in front of him. He knew the two men were still inside the room with him. But after experiencing a few minutes in the dark, he was no longer sure. There was no movement, no noise. Just the eerie deafness of silence. It was at that moment when he realized something very profound; when you are alone in the dark and your life is on the line, the mind has a funny way of playing tricks on you.

As Tyrone began to feed off of his own thoughts, he began to reflect on his past and regretted the way he had lived his life. He couldn't help but wonder what his life would have been like if things were different? He thought about marriage, children and a mindless nine-to-five he knew he would have hated. Instead, he was being held captive and was probably about to be tortured for information he knew he could not provide.

He began to dwell on the word, torture and had to question his inner strength. He had no idea what his tolerance for pain was, and knew he could take an ass-whipping, but torture, he wasn't so sure.

As he sat there wondering what they were going to do with him? He cringed at the thought of what they were capable of. He have never been a religious man, but for some reason he thought a silent prayer might be appropriate and found himself appealing to his higher power. "Not the nuts, lord. Please not the nuts," was his idea of appealing to a higher power. He thought about the call he had made to SunRise and wished someone had answered the phone. He never got a chance to write down the address of the apartment building, and wasn't even sure if he was at the same apartment building he had been surveying before his abduction. He thought about it and realized, even if he had gotten through to SunRise and manage to give him the address to where he was being held. No one had any way of knowing which apartment he was being held at.

As he continued wrestling with his thoughts, he heard some footsteps. His head immediately turned in the direction of the sound. He then heard a squeaky noise just before the blindfold  was snatched from around his eyes. The room was dark except for a small lamp that hung from the ceiling directly over the chair in which he sat. He noticed a window directly behind the desk. No curtains, just wood blinds that were pulled close. There was a shadowy man sitting behind the desk, watching. He couldn't quite make out the man's face, just an outline. Slim built, slick hair, suit-jacket, shirt and tie. He was leaning back in a swivel desk-chair that squeaks as he moved in it. His hands were coupled behind his neck. Feet planted on top of the desk resting comfortably on what looked like a huge folder. There was also a phone, gun, and something else on the desk. Tyrone looked at the suit standing behind him. Then at the shadowy suit standing by the door. He rubbed and rotated his jaw. It was throbbing along with the left side of his face. "You wanna' tell me why you had me dragged out of my car, beaten and brought here? Who the fuck are you people?"

"Don't you know, Mr..." he shift his feet to the other side to gain access to the folder in front of him. "...Oh yes. Here we go," he began breezing through the file. "... Sharp, is it?" he paused momentarily before continuing. "Who sometimes go by the name, Tyrone Shurp." He sat the file back on the desk and looked at Tyrone. "Very clever, tweaking your name. I have to remember that one. Now, you want to tell me why a man like you think you can fuck with a man like me?" he immediately changed the subject.

"What? Mannn, I don't even know you. And I damn sure don't know what the hell you're talking about?"

"According to your lawyer, Mr. Vincent is it? Yes... well... he has been very cooperative in providing us with quite extensive intel' on you and of course the other members of your little organization."

"Look here, man. I don't have a clue what the hell you're talking about!"

The suit who had been standing behind Tyrone, immediately grabbed him by the throat and looked at his employer for approval. The man sitting behind the desk held up his hand, giving the suit the 'stop' sign. The suit then released Tyrone neck and returned to his former position. Tyrone rubbed his throat and coughed in an effort to catch his breath.

"I apologize for my associate. He sometimes gets a little impetuous. Now... where were we?" He scanned through the file until he found what he had been looking for. Then looks up from the file at Tyrone. "Do you have any idea how much money you've cost me. How much time and man-power I've wasted trying to track you and your..." he paused, looked at the ceiling while rubbing his chin with his index finger and thumb. "...what would be the appropriate word? Comrades. Yes, I think comrades will do. What do you think, Mr. Sharp?"

"I think you lost your damn mind!"

"WRONG ANSWER!" he shouted while removing his feet from the desk to sit up straight. The suit who had been standing behind Tyrone immediately placed his gun to Tyrone's head and cocked a round in the chamber. "But you are about to lose yours if you don't tell me what I want to know." He clicked his  finger and the room immediately  filled with light.

Tyrone squinted from the sudden burst of brightness until his eyes finally adjusted. That's when he saw the .45 automatic the suit standing behind him was aiming at his head. He then looked at the man sitting behind the desk and now had a face to go with the voice. Tyrone thought the man looked like something straight out of a GQ magazine. Not only was he impeccably dressed, but also well groomed. Tyrone figured he was either in his mid or late thirties. He also noticed his gun, and wallet sitting on top of the desk along with a huge folder underneath the man's Louis Vuitton loafers. At least Tyrone had assume they were, Vuitton's? It was the designer's red sole signature that led Tyrone to such a conclusion.

The moment the man saw Tyrone eyeing his things, he picked up the wallet and began fishing through it. Tyrone watched as he pulls out what looks like his driver's licenses and tosses it on the desk before poking further. Tyrone glanced at the suit and the gun he held to his head. There was a suppresser attached to the large weapon which wasn't a good sign. Tyrone wasn't sure why he was being detained by Mr. GQ and his suits, and wasn't about to die without finding out.

"You mind if I ask who you are and what you want with me?"

Still going through the wallet, Mr. GQ began to speak without taking his eyes from the items he pulls out of the wallet. "I would like to make something very clear so there will be no misunderstanding, Mr. Sharp. Who I am is of no importance, nor is how you managed to find out about my shipment in, Queens. What is, however, are the copies of that disk you stole? And before you open your mouth with something clever to say. Consider this, I am not just going to kill you, Mr. Sharp.

I am going to kill everyone you've ever known and loved." He sat the wallet down and looked at Tyrone with a stern gaze. Then grabbed the file in front of him and began scanning through the pages. "I know everything about you and I do mean everything."

Tyrone frowned. "Mannn! I don't know what the hell my lawyer, Mr. Vincent told you, but he's a damn lie!"

He smiles with wicked thin lips and said, "The copies, Mr. Sharp. Where are the copies you and your friends made of my disk?"

"Ain't no damn copies! I gave that thing to my lawyer, end of story." He studied Tyrone's face briefly and was about to speak but was interrupted when the phone, sitting on top of the desk began to ring. All eyes looked at the phone. "You gonna' get that, or should I?" asked Tyrone.

Clearly upset by the sudden interruption, he snatched up the receiver. YES!" he angrily yelled into the receiver. Tyrone watched as his expression changed from annoyance, to that of concern. "WHO IS THIS!" he shouted again. A few seconds later, his face went flush and his demeanor change. He then looked at Tyrone and uttered under his breath, "She wants to speak with you," while handing over the phone. Both suits looked at one another, confused.

Tyrone slowly stood and walked up to the desk and took the phone from him. "What's up?"

"Leave why you still can," said the female's voice before abruptly hanging up. Unable to identify the woman's voice, Tyrone slowly hung up the receiver and began gathering up his things from on top of the desk. He glanced at the well groomed man who just sat there watching while he grabbed his wallet along with several other important papers that had been removed from his wallet. Tyrone looked at the file sitting on the desk, then at his well dressed capture and said, "I believe this belongs to me," while grabbing the file. The well dressed man stared at him with such hostility, Tyrone could smell the hatred leaking from his pores. Tyrone smiled nervously and wanted to talk shit, but didn't want to over play his hand. After all, he wasn't out of the woods just yet. He had no idea who the woman on the phone was and didn't care. One thing was for sure, he thought. Whoever she was? It would seem  Mr. GQ  definitely had a tremendous amount of respect for her.

As soon as Tyrone reached for his gun on top of the desk, both of the suits cocks and aimed their weapon at him. "NO!" shouted their boss while holding both hands out in an effort to get the two suits to stand down. Tyrone froze and heard something whiz passed his face twice. Both of the suits heads exploded. Tyrone watched in horror as the two men bodies dropped like three-hundred-pound bags of solid concrete, dead.

Shocked by such a gruesome sight. Tyrone stared at the two dead bodies that were missing half of their heads and cried out, "OH SHIT! WHAT THE FUCK!" When he turned and face the man sitting at the desk. He noticed the holes in the wood blinders behind the man's desk. "Yo, man?" he nervously began. "The woman on the phone said I could leave?"

Sitting completely still as if afraid to move, the well dressed man angrily shouted, "THAN LEAVE!" Piece of chipped wood from the blinder littered his hair, shoulders and desk- top.

Tyrone quickly grabbed the gun from the desk and headed for the door while tucking it in his waist. The moment he opened the door, he was inimically greeted by three more suits with weapons drawn. Tyrone raised both hand into the air and shouted, "WAIT!" The suits looked at their boss for direction, but it was too late. Several more bullets whizzed past Tyrone's head again and found their target into the torsos of the three suits.

Once the shooting stopped, Tyrone turned and looked at the man who had not moved from his desk. The room was now dark again, but Tyrone could still see his shadow sitting behind the desk, motionless. He is gazing back at Tyrone with little slits for eyes. Behind him is a single infrared beam of light moving throughout the room from the window as if trying to find it's next target. "Aw damn!" Tyrone signed. The wood blinders that once provided a level of privacy has been completely ripped away by the recent onslaught of heavy caliber bullets.

"Leave, Mr. Sharp. You can find your way out down the steps to your right."

"You ain't gotta' tell me twice. Um' gone." It took Tyrone a minute or so, but he finally managed to find his way out of the huge, plush apartment.

Once he was inside his car, he tossed the file on the passenger seat and sat there for a moment trying to collect himself. He couldn't believe how close he had come to dying. It was an experience he had no desire to repeat.

Johnathen Crain Jr. was still sitting at his desk in the study when Roger Ross walked in. Armed with a Smith & Wesson, he looked at his boss and said, "All clear, sir." Then led Crain out of the room while three of his men continue to carefully check the perimeter.

Ross and his boss were standing in the living-room when one of the men came in. "Looks like a single shooter. As far as I can tell, they used a 50-cal. Won't know for sure until I check the shells. The shots were fire from one of the buildings across the street. You want us to take a look, Sir?"

"No," Ross told him. "The shooter is long gone by now. But Mr. Sharp? I'm sure we should be able to catch up with him," he muttered before shouting, "You two," he ordered. "Take the jeep and take him out. We're looking for a white 1991 BMW. License T-Y-E-1."

Both men nodded and immediately left the apartment. Ross then looked at his young boss, Crain, and asked, "Is there anything you can tell me about the female's voice, Sir?"

Clearly on edge, Crain quickly fixed himself a glass of Scotch and sat on the sofa. "I didn't hear a single shot?" he said in a daze-like state. "She had to be one of Sharp's people. What do we do now?"

"I've lost five men tonight. Hilton was a good man. Whoever the shooter was? Is going to pay. I think it's about time we start applying our own brand of pressure, don't you?"

"You don't expect me to believe all those shots came from one rifle, do you?"

"Looks that way, Mr. Crain. Looks like the work of a sniper. Either way, we're up against professionals. I'll have someone come to remove the bodies and clean this mess up. In the mean time, I have to get you out of here.

Roger Ross was a tall, thin, but solidly built man under the dark gray suit he wore. Pale in complexion, he was a clean shaven man with very bad facial skin from shaving not only too close, but too often as well. The pot-holes in his face from the ingrown hairs was a testament to that fact.

Ross wore his grayish, sandy-blond hair close to lighten the impact of his receding hair-line. Which made him appeared older than his actual age. Ex-military, he led a 'Special Forces' unit in Saigon during the 'Vietnam War' in the late 1960's. After the war was over, Ross, along with what was left of his unit, returned to the States. Patriots to the core, they had all expected to be warmly greeted by grateful Americans whose freedom they fought to protect. Instead, they came home to thousands of angry protesters shouting the unthinkable while spiting on them. It was a bad time for everyone. Ross and his men not only returned home to hostile anti-war protesters, but were unable to find decent work. A few of them even tried re-enlisting, but the war was over and without the action, it just wasn't the same.

Ross was well aware of the hard time his former squad had been having adjusting to civilian life, and knew that could never be him. For him, there was only one alternative and that was to do what he knew best. Search and destroy.

By the early 1970s, Roger Ross finally found a place for himself in mainstream society in the security profession. After managing to save enough money 'baby-sitting' rich actors and rock-stars. He began to pick-and-choose assignments that he felt best suited him. It wasn't long before meeting an old, rich, businessman by the name of, Johnathen Crain who had been having trouble with one of his business associates. A ruthless female crime-lord named, Patti Johnson. Ross didn't know that much about her except the fact that she was a South American and had a propensity for murdering her enemies. As soon as Johnathen Crain heard about Ross' secrete talents, he immediately hired Ross and made him head of his security. But by then, Patti had the FBI on her tail and disappeared like a puff of smoke. Leaving an indelible fear in the hearts of those who crossed her path. Ross and his men never had the pleasure of locking horns with the female crime-lord.

More than twenty years had passed since the days of Patti Johnson. After Johnathen Crain lost his wife to cancer. He lost his drive for business and allowed a close friend and business partner to run Crain Industries, the empire he built from the ground up. As his health began to deteriorate, he felt he no longer had a need for a man like Ross and introduced him to his son.

Junior was a prominent attorney and junior associate at a reputable New York law firm. At first, Junior did not feel he had a need for a security team. His father, nevertheless, had been insistent. Schooling Junior to the chronicles of Patti Johnson. After reluctantly interviewing Ross as a favor to his father. Junior was impressed with Ross' credentials, whose resume read like a 'soldier of fortune'. Junior not only hired Roger Ross on the spot, but also made him head of security. With the promise of a handsome salary, Ross accept Junior's offer on one condition? He be allowed to personally choose his own team. Once Junior agreed, it was a match.

On the parkway heading north, Tyrone got a call on his car phone from the unknown female. "Don't look now," said the caller, "but you have a tail closing in on you, fast." When Tyrone glanced in his rearview and spotted the white Cherokee coming up behind him. He quickly pulled out his nine and cocked it while changing lanes. He tried to put a few cars between him and his pursuers but it didn't work. Within seconds, the white jeep was on his left side. He could see the man on the passenger side of the jeep cocking what looked like a .45 automatic. But before he got the opportunity to point and shoot. Tyrone rolled down his window, took aim and shot first, "POP-POP-POP!" The jeep swerved off to the far left and slowed down while Tyrone quickly navigated his 'Beamer' all the way to the right. Giving him plenty of time to lose the white jeep. He wasn't sure if he actually hit his target and didn't care. He was just happy to be clear of those men.

Once Tyrone arrived back in Paterson, it was much too late to call, or try to see Catherine. Still, he vowed, at first light he was going to make a concerted effort to see what kind of fool she had taken him for.

# CHAPTER 8

All the lights were out when Camille returned to the suite late that evening. The place seemed lonely and abandoned without the company of someone to return home to. She thought about Vicki and didn't really expect her to still be there. Not after the fight they'd had earlier. She silently cursed herself for being so hard on her only because she knew she could have handled the situation a little better and had no one to blame but herself.

After closing the door behind her, she dropped the large duffel at the door and walked over to the sofa. Before sitting, she tossed the folder onto the coffee table, slipped out of her coat and sat to remove her knee high boots. She smiled at the thought of Vicki helping her out of her boots earlier. She thought about how broken Vicki seemed and regretted the way she had treated her. Once she finally had both boots off, she sat there for a moment, or so, rubbing her feet while still thinking about Vicki. She wanted to kick herself in the ass. Mostly for losing her temper earlier. She stood and walked straight to the bathroom where she undressed until she was completely nude. After brushing her teeth, she took a quick hot shower. It had been a long day and she was tired. Ten minutes later, she stepped out of the shower and proceeded to dry off. She stepped out of the bathroom and noticed, for the first time, Vicki lying in bed asleep. A warm feeling came over her.

While tip-toeing around the bed-area to avoid waking Vicki. She gathered a few thing she needed to groom, then stood in front of the dresser-mirror and began to lotion her entire body. Once she was done, she quietly stepped back into the living area and sat on the large sofa with her legs folded to the side under her. She could still see Vicki in the dark from where she sat and could not take her eyes off of her.

Finally mustering enough courage. She walked into the bed-area and sat on the side of the bed. That's when she noticed Vicki's cloths, including her underwear, neatly fold and placed in a chair in the sitting area by the window.

When she looked at Vicki again, Vicki woke and looked up at her. Camille forced a weak, but gentle smile. "Did I wake you?" she softly asked.

"No," Vicki replied.

"Feel lil' better now?" Camille gently stroked the side of Vicki's face with the back of her hand.

"Lil' bit, thanks," Vicki said before apologizing. "I'm sorry for trying to fork you earlier. Don't know where that came from?"

"Shhh. You don't have to apologize. I'm here for you. "Camille whispered in a caring manner while easing under the covers beside her. Vicki's body felt warm as Camille held her in her arms the way a mother holds her child and gently stroked her face.

"I've never felt so alone," Vicki continued. Camille felt nothing but empathy for her. Having suffered similar loses in the past, she completely understood what Vicki was going through. "I can't believe they both gone," Vicki muttered. "I miss 'em both so much," her lips quivered and her words cracked into a series of sobs.

"Shhh, shhh. You'll be a'ight, Vicki. You got me," Camille spoke softly with a hoodish, southern slur while lifting Vicki's head to look at her in the dark. As Vicki stared into her eyes, Camille continued. "We have each other." She brought her lips to Vicki's face and lightly kissed her on her tear-stained cheek. Vicki's grief had left her vulnerable. Camille had pushed all the right buttons, and said all the right things. Things Vicki needed to hear. She was hurting, feeling lost and alone. She needed to be consoled, held, kissed and told everything was going to be all right. With her sister, husband and mother-in-law now gone. There was a void in her life. A void that needed to be filled. Camille was determined to fill that void. She knew exactly what Vicki had been through and what she was going through. She became the shoulder to cry on. The someone to hold her, kiss her, love her, and possibly make love to her.

Camille was still asleep when Vicki woke. It was early. About five in the morning and raining outside. Aside from the throbbing pain from the gunshot wound she sustained the night she lost her husband. Vicki felt well rested and less depressed about the lost of her husband and mother-in-law. The world seemed quiet and at peace as she laid there watching Camille snore quietly next to her.

113

She thought about her sister, Vanessa and realized how much she had missed her. In a way, she regretted not driving down to Camden to see her before they moved her. But also knew her sister would have understood if she knew why Vicki chose not to make the trip to see her one last time.

Vicki looked at the woman lying next to her and wondered about her ethnic background? When she first saw Camille, she had just assumed Camille was Latino. After hearing her speak, she was no longer sure. Now looking at her, she appeared to be white in a Middle-eastern sort of way.

Vicki closed her eyes and tried to drift back off to sleep, but began thinking about Londell instead. She still had trouble believing he was gone and knew no man could ever take his place. In bed he was a forceful brut who knew what she wanted and how she wanted it. The mere thought of never having him screwing her brains out sadden her to no end. She thought about the first time they made love. He was hardly her type and the last person she envisioned herself with. Even after he had saved her from those murdering rapists, the only thing she remembered feeling for him was gratitude. As a matter of fact, the only reason she ultimately gave him some was because she thought she would use her hot-pocket as a tool to ensure him teaching her the murder game. It was only after sampling his package and skills, she was only too proud to claim him as her man. She cuddled up against Camille's naked warm body under the thick blanket and closed her eyes. Secretly imagining it was his body next to her. As the pain from her wound subsided, she slowly drifted back off to sleep.

Camille was a veteran at fulfilling certain needs and Vicki was an easy read. She provided exactly what Vicki needed in more way then one. Having lost so much in such a short period of time, Camille knew Vicki was vulnerable. She also knew Vicki was experiencing guilt and shame. Guilt because deep down, she felt responsible for her husband's death. Shame because it was her arrogance that caused her to underestimate the targets. It was the perfect opportunity for Camille to exploit Vicki's weaknesses. But first, she had to brake her spirit. Which meant pressing the right buttons to push her over the edge. Vicki's guilt was the common denominator. By accusing Vicki of being responsible for her husband's death, Camille managed to reduce Vicki to the lowest term. Then, moved in for the kill by being attentive, nurturing, and caring just when Vicki needed someone to be.

Two hours and fifteen minutes later, both women woke. Laying side by side in silence, neither one of them spoke for different reasons. Vicki, because there were no words for what they had done last night. Feeling a little awkward, she looked at Camille but did not know what to say, or if she should say anything at all. Camille on the other hand felt she had moved a little too fast last night. Vicki was hurting and in pain. Instead  of consoling her, she took advantage of Vicki's vulnerability to fulfill her own selfish needs.

"I  want to apologize again for trying to fork you yesterday." Vicki finally broke the silence.

Camille looked at her and smiled. "I should be the one apologizing. You had every right to be upset, even a lil' suspicious. I shouldn't have left you in suspense like that, or  said those nasty things about you. And for that, I apologize."

Vicki thought about it and wanted to know what Camille really thought about her. "Did you mean what you said about me?" she asked, avoiding eye contact as Camille answered.

Camille turned on her belly and looked at Vicki. "No. And I'm sorry if what I said hurt you, but you hurt me, too. I was just trying to get back at you."

Surprised by Camille's response, Vicki had to ask, "How in the world did I hurt you?"

"By rudely interrupting me while I was trying to explain how we met."

Vicki's eyes softened. "Oh, yeah. I'm sorry. I wasn't trying to be rude, or anything. I just had a lot of other things on my mind."

"I know. You don't have to go back to that horrible place and time. I'm here for you, if you want me to be?"

A lost for words, Vicki eyed Camille with a curiosity. "Thank you. You've been very nice to me."

Camille crawled on top of Vicki's chest and gazed into her eyes. "I want to be more?" she said.

Vicki knew where the conversation was going. Where Camille was trying to take it. "What did you mean when you said you saved my ass the night my man was killed? Were you there?" Vicki immediately changed the subject.

Camille took a deep breath and exhaled slowly. "That's how we met. I was the one at the door, remember?"

Vicki eyes widen with shock as she pushed Camille off of her. Without saying a word, she stared at Camille with angry narrowing eyes.

"The name of the man who attacked you inside Henderson's house and murdered your husband was Spurlock. He worked for a man by the name of Johnathen Crain Junior," Camille quickly spoke up.

Vicki sat up. "That was you who answered the door that night," she stated with horror while remembering. "You...."

"Saved your life!" Camille quickly interrupted her. "I'm sorry about your boyfriend, but the way you were handling yourself? I was sure you could take him. By the time I realized what was happening, he had already pushed your boyfriend and..."

"Husband," Vicki corrected her.

Camille look at Vicki's ring finger and didn't see a wedding band, "...had a gun to your head and was about to pull the trigger. I pushed him before he had a chance to push you."

"You? I thought Tyrone Sharp helped me?"

"Tyrone Sharp?"

117

"Yeah. You know him?"

"No."

"He works for the person who contracted me and my husband for the Henderson job," Vicki said while laying down again. "I remember watching that man  murder Londell. I must have passed out after that because the only thing I remember is waking up at a safe-house. I really fucked up. Londell tried to tell me to wear a vest, "Don't underestimate the target," he told me, but I was too full of myself."

"STOP IT!" Camille jumped in. "First of all, you and your husband were out of your league. The man you encounter at the house was a professional killer who enjoyed his work a little too much for me. Y'all just happen to show up at the wrong time, that's all. My intentions were to get rid of you at the door, but you forced your way in. After that, it was too late."

As Vicki remembered, she realized she had no one to blame but herself. She didn't want to think about it anymore and was beginning to regret bringing it up. "If you're ready to finish telling me about your past. I'm ready to listen?" she changed the subject with hopes of taking her mind off of that terrible night.

"You promise not to interrupt me this time?" Camille playfully asked while sitting on the edge of the bed.

"I promise," Vicki said  before sitting up to get comfortable.

"Where was I?"

"You said something about after you were born?"

"Oh, yeah," Camille said as she remembered. "I was the daughter of a single parent home, if you wanna' call the streets home. I was told my mother came from wealthy parents who, if I'm not mistaken, still resides in the French Quarter in New Orleans. I was also told my grandparents were direct descendants of the original settlers of Louisiana. Unfortunately, the moment they learned their precious little daughter was pregnant with me. They completely disowned her and denied any existence of me." Camille smiled as she remembered. "My mom was a beautiful woman before she became overwhelmed by the streets. Everyone called her Frenchie. A nickname given to her by the mean streets of the 'Ninth Ward' in the Middle Town section of New Orleans. After she became strung-out, it wasn't long before she found herself working cheap motel in the Quarters. Much later after I was born, her stomping ground became the Ninth Ward. My life came to a cross-road when I met, Jaedm. I couldn't have been no more than six at the time. I was dirty, tired, and hungry. Frenchie had been dragging me around all day from one hell-hole to the next. It was late. About two in the morning and I had been sitting alone outside of this raggedy-ass single room motel for hours waiting on my mom. There were no lights outside of the motel rooms. It was dark, in a creepy sort of way. The good thing was; I could see if someone approached, but no one could see me sitting there in the dark. So, for the most part, I felt safe. Anyway, while I was dozing off, I heard a noise that sound something like a series of sneezes. I looked around and saw a light coming from a room about four or five rooms down. The door was open and someone was about to come out. I remember hoping it was one of the working girls who knew me and my mom. When I saw a man come out, I remembered being disappointed. He tuck something in the waist of his pant, then pulled his shirt over the front to conceal it and lit a cigarette. As he stood there pulling on the cigarette. I prayed he went the other way. When he start walking in my direction, I put my head down, hoping he wouldn't notice me. As luck would have it, he stops right in front of me. "What you doing out here this time of night, lil' girl?" he asked me. I told him I was waiting for my mom. "Where she at?" he asked. With my back to the filthy door behind me, I nodded towards the door to indicate she was inside. "You live there?" I didn't answer. I just wanted him to leave, but when he asked me was I hungry? I looked up at him. My eyes must of lit up like flood-lights searching for a meal because he notice and smiled. "Wait here," he said. I watched him walk down to the parking-lot and get something out of a car. When he returned, he had a greasy paper bag. "Here you go," he said while handing me the bag. I all but snatched it out of his hand and clasped it tightly to my lil' chest. He stood there smiling. "Ain't you gonna' eat it?" he asked. I just looked at him hoping he would hurry up and leave so I could satisfy the hunger pains that cramped my stomach. "Well ain't you gonna' at least say, thank you?"

Afraid to look at him, I held my head down and said, "Thank you, mis'tah." He then asked me what my name was? I looked at him and said, "Camille."

He smiled and said, "Enjoy the meal, Cami," then left.

I frowned and shouted after him. "My name Camille! Not Cami!" but he never turned around. I don't think he heard me.

Around ten that morning, two known hoods and two prostitutes were found shot to death in the same room I watched him come out of. One of the prostitutes turned out to be the niece of some politician who must have been complaining because the police were desperate to make an arrest. They kept sweating all the known prostitutes in the area until somebody told them something. Someone finally did. It was two prostitutes who had been sitting in a car in the lot at the time. They must have saw him talking to me because they told the police they saw a known thug talking to some lil' girl around the same time the coroner gave the time of death. One of the women even picked Jaedm out of a line-up. Four hours later she was found dead. Shot in the head twice and once in the mouth. But the D.A. had another card to play? The lil' girl who had been seen talking to Jaedm. Because I was the only child at the motel that night, the D.A. began pressuring Frenchie about allowing their psyche to interview me. When Frenchie refused. They told her they could arrest her for 'endangering the welfare of a child' and threatened to place me in Child Care. At that point, Frenchie agreed on one condition? They place the both of us in protective custody. They agreed and an appointment was immediately set up to have their psyche interview me. The interview was based on credibility. They wanted to see if I had any credible information that would help their case. After the interview, I was deemed credible, but the information I gave totally destroyed the state's case against the man they had in custody. Jaedm was light-skinned, short, stocky, wore his head clean shaven. The description I gave was a tall, dark-skinned man who wore his hair in an afro."

Vicki was smiling now. "What they do?" she quickly asked while adding, "They had to be pissed!"

"Pissed ain't the word. They were seething. The material witness warrant was lifted and Frenchie and I were kicked to the curb. Which was fine with the both of us."

"You ever see him again?"

"Yeah. About six years later after Frenchie was murdered."

"What?"

"But that's another story."

"You mean to tell me you're not going to finish?"

"I would, but I have to be someplace and right now I'm late." Camille rolled out of bed, walked into the front room and placed a black leather duffel in the closet before returning to the bedroom.

Vicki was still lying in bed when she asked, "When you gonna' finish your story?"

"When I get back."

Vicki looked at her watch. "But it's not even eight yet?" she whined.

"You gonna' be here when I get back?"

"I guess. I don't have any place else to go, except back to my mother-in-law. Ain't nothing left for me there except my things. I also wanna' find out about the funeral, you know? If there's anything I can do to help?"

"You going?" Camille casually asked while moving around the large room as if she was in a hurry.

"I haven't decided yet," Vicki replied.

"Well, whatever you decide, I'm here for you," Camille said before sashaying off to the bathroom.

As Vicki laid there thinking about her current situation. She couldn't help wondering about Camille's ulterior motive and began to feel 'some-kind-of-way'. Since leaving home, the only people she met who actually didn't want anything from her where now dead. Just as she was about to get out of bed, the pain from her wound shot threw her entire body. She slowly sat up and carefully removed the bandage in the front. Then the one in the back just to make sure she hadn't busted any stitches. The pain was almost intolerable, but nothing was more painful than the two people she had just lost.

When Camille came out of the bathroom, she immediately noticed Vicki's discomfort. "You a'ight?" she asked.

"Yeah. It's this wound. Shit hurts like hell."

Camille looked at both sides of the wound. "You didn't rupture any stitches and it seems to be healing nicely. Don't cover it up anymore.

It'll heal faster if you allow it to breathe. Do you have anything for the pain?"

"Everything Doc gave me are at my mother-in-law's."

Somewhat concerned, Camille stared at Vicki and asked, "You think you'll be a'ight 'til you can get to your medication? 'Cause fuck what I have to do, that shit ain't as important. If need be, I'll run out this mutha' right now and find my baby something to ease her pain, you hear me?"

Vicki giggled. "I heard. I'll be a'ight."

"You sure?"

"Yeah. I'm good."

"Okay, baby." Camille sat on the side of the bed and leaned close to Vicki's face. "I'll let the bitch at the desk know I have a guest staying with me. That way you won't have any problems getting pass her when you get back. See you later, Okay?" Without waiting for an answer. She leaned in to kiss Vicki on the lips but Vicki slightly turned her face. The kiss landed on her cheek instead. Camille smiled and walked off into the living area. Vicki watched her pick something up from the coffee table and retrieve the black duffel from the closet before leaving the suite.

# CHAPTER 9

Tyrone didn't get much sleep after arriving back in Paterson. He jumped at every little sound. Rushing over to the window to peek out each time he heard a car outside passing by. What he had went through last night was enough excitement to last him a lifetime. The extent of his physical injuries were minor compared to the psychological damage that traumatize him. Still, that did not stop him from calling Doc. Who immediately took one look at Tyrone's face and applied some antiseptic. Then finished up by applying a band-aid over the small opened wound. The swelling had went down considerably since last night. Doc gave him some pain pills and a clean bill of health before leaving. Tyrone thought about what Mr. G.Q. said about his lawyer, Melvin Vincent who, according to Mr. G.Q., sold them out. He tried calling the New York branch attorney but the number was no longer listed. He knew SunRise knew more than he was telling him and didn't like being kept in the dark one bit. He thought about TooSweet and suddenly began to worry. Mainly because, as far as he knew, no one have seen or heard anything from her except Mr. Vincent. Which made him worry for her safety now more than ever. He looked around the small apartment for the Intel' file those men had on him, but couldn't find it anywhere. He remembered taking it but after that, nothing? "Think, Tyrone! Think!" he told himself while trying to recall the events after the shooting stopped. Again, he drew a blank. Desperate to know what was in the file, he thought back before the shooting and remembered taking the file from the desk, but just couldn't remember what he did with it afterwards. He thought about SunRise and couldn't wait to tell him what he had been through. He tried calling several times, but had been unable to reach him. He thought about Catherine Henderson and had to admit, she was good. The story she gave him concerning why she had left her husband was very convincing. He remembered Renee' telling him about Catherine's infidelity and wondered? He couldn't wait to speak with her again. Mostly about her relationship with those men?

Before hitting the streets this time, Tyrone made certain he was prepared. Armed with a twelve round, semi automatic nine millimeter and two back-up clips. He put on a carbon fiber 'Dragon skin' bulletproof-vest before slipping on his sweater and coat. He was sure the suits who chased him last night knew what kind of car he was driving. Which meant using his car would be a bad idea. He was about to call a cab when all of a sudden, his phone began to ring. "Yeah?"

"It's me," said the caller.

He immediately recognized SunRise's voice, and shouted, "FINALLY!" before continuing. "Rise, man. I've been trying to get a hold of you all morning. You ain't gonna' believe the shit I've been through," he said without giving the caller a chance to get one word in. "What? I'm at the safe-house on North Main. Mannn, I was kidnapped last night. Um' lucky to be alive. What? Oh, a'ight. I'll be here. Please hurry up, yo."

While awaiting SunRise's arrival, he began pacing. Every now and then he would glance at his watch wondering what was taking SunRise so long?

Thirteen minutes later, SunRise stood at the door shaking rain-water from his umbrella before stepping into the house. Tyrone was beside himself and began rambling on about his horrendous ordeal last night. He never noticed the small leather folder SunRise was carrying. "Yo, where the hell you been, Rise? Look at my face, yo. I've been beaten and kidnapped.

"By who?"

"Some young white cat who looked like he could of been a model for G.Q. magazine. He and his suits tried to push me, man. Kept asking me 'bout copies of the disk you had me send to Mr. Vincent. Who, by the way, crossed us. That ass-hole Crain had a file on me. He said Mr. Vincent gave it to him. He said he have files on all of us? You cool, though. Vincent didn't know anything about you."

Without saying a word, SunRise sat at the table in the dinning-room and opened the case. As he rambled through the contents, Tyrone continued to beat him down about his ordeal last night. Once SunRise found what he had been looking for, he showed it to Tyrone. It was a photo-copy of a newspaper clipping of the man who had kidnap and questioned Tyrone last night.

"THAT'S HIM!" Tyrone shouted. He then looked at SunRise somewhat confused. "Who the hell is he, 'Rise?"

"Someone whose name is also on the disk. I had him checked out. His name is Johnathen Crain Jr. and his father owns Crain Industries."

"Never heard of 'em?" said Tyrone.

It didn't surprise SunRise in the least. People like the Crains; people from 'old money' were never interested in publicity. Just making money the old fashion way, stealing it. "Young Crain is a successful lawyer with one of New York's prestigious law firms. Ledet, Stockwell & Mann. As a favor to his father, the firm recruited Junior straight out of Law school with the assurance that they would move him where the money was being made. Civil litigation. Instead, they buried him in criminal law."

"So he's a criminal attorney?"

"I imagine he hated it at first, but probably didn't have a say in the matter. Remember, it was his father who got him the job in the first place. I suspect he swallowed his pride until his time came. I'm guessing that's when he met Teflon Figueroa."

"The same guy you had Black-Sun watch?"

"That be him. His uncle is Hector Figueroa, but no one has made a connection between Tef' and his uncle's Dominican cartel."

"I never heard of his uncle, or a damn Dominican cartel? Mexican and Colombian yeah, but not no damn Dominican," said Tyrone before adding, "You mean to tell me that lil' young ass cat balling like that? He sure ain't look like no baller in the photo I gave Black-Sun?"

"You slipping, Tye. After Junior met Teflon, he came up in less than two years. New position as a Junior-partner with stock options, a corner office overlooking the Hudson River and an attractive assistant he personally handpicked. Guess who the assistant was?"

"Please don't tell me, Catherine Henderson?"

"Exactly."

"So Mike met her though that lawyer dude who's trying to end us?"

"That I couldn't tell you. All I know is, Teflon isn't just a cocaine broker from Washington Heights. He was Mike's supplier and apparently friends with Mike's wife long before Mike ever knew her."

"I talked to this sista' last night who knows Mike's wife, and she had some messed up things to say about her?"

"What exactly did she say about her?"

"That she played the shit out of Mike."

"How?"

Tyrone laughed as he remembered. "She said, before he got with his wife, he was doing all right copping three or four birds at a time. His wife talked him into copping on consignment."

SunRise was silently thinking. In spite of what everyone had told him about Michael Henderson's wife, he now had every reason to believe she was not his mystery woman at the Henderson's house that night.

"You think she was telling me the truth, or talking just to be talking?" Tyrone asked in search of a little more insight. "Renee got her information from one of Mike's boys. Jokers be telling her all kinda' stuff. She said she'll bet anything Mike's wife set him up from the rip. She seems to think Mike's wife was up to something. Personally, I think Renee was reaching on that one. She can't stand Mike's wife. Probably 'cause she white?"

"Never underestimate people, Tye. Who knows what this woman is capable of? If what your friend said about her is true? She must have arranged to have young Crain provided the bank, Teflon the product and brought Mike in to provide the muscle to push the product for Crain Junior. Looks to me like she tried to do the three of them a favor by making them all rich." SunRise thought about it again. "What I don't understand is, what was she suppose to get out of it? You said she tried to set you up last night?"

"Hell yeah! I know she put Crain's bulls on me. Can you believe that? Told me she didn't know nothing about Mike's affairs. I believed her, too. I was about to leave when I saw her point me out to Crain's men. I broke. They musta' thought I was gone, 'cause they jumped in this brand new white Cherokee but didn't leave. I saw your boy, Asmar walk right up to the jeep and told them something before they left. I followed them to an apartment in lower Manhattan, that's when I called you. The next thing I knew, someone clocked me. I woke in this big ass apartment where they started questioning me about copies of the disk. Your boy Crain sitting behind this big ass cherry-wood desk going through my wallet. I was cursing his ass out when all of a sudden his phone rings. He snatches up the receiver to answer it. He was pissed, 'Rise. You shoulda' seem 'em. Whoever it was musta' scared him to DEATH! Because after that, his expression changed from pissed to scared-shitless. He looked at me and said, "she wants to speak to you.""

"She?" SunRise quickly asked.

"Yeah, some female. I took the phone and said, "Yeah, what's up?" Some female on the line told me to leave. Brutha', I grabbed my lil' things from off the top of Crain's desk but as soon as I reached for my piece, all hell broke loose. Both of Crain's suits pulled out on me. Crain shouted, "NO!" but it was too late. Someone from the building across the street start shooting. I still can't believe I wasn't hit. Bullets buzzed past my head like honey-bees on a mission. Whoever she was? Didn't just saved my ass, she took out every suit Crain had up in there. I don't know what kinda' caliber she used, but that shit spit lead through walls." Tyrone paused briefly before asking, "You think it could have been Mike's wife?"

"No. I don't. What was Crain doing when the shooting started?"

"He never moved from his desk. I knew he was scared but I didn't realize why until everyone else ended up dead. During the shooting, the bullets must of taken out the light in the room because before leaving, I saw this infrared moving through the room like it was about to take out the first thing that moved." He paused in thought for a moment. "Oh, yeah! Something else happened. While I was on the parkway heading back to Paterson. I get a call on my car-phone from the same female. How the hell she got my number is beyond me. She said, "Don't look now, but you have a tail closing in on you." Two more suits driving that white Cherokee tried to push me on the parkway. Once they were close enough, I shot at them. I don't know if I hit anything but it slowed them down long enough for me to shake 'em. I can't wait to see that woman, Catherine, again. I got some choice words for her."

"When you talked to her on the phone, did she sound like Henderson's wife?"

"Naw'. Not at all. You don't have any idea who she could have been, 'Rise?"

"No, but who ever she is? She moves like a spook, and according to you, fights like a professional." SunRise thought for a moment before adding, "If its the same person, she seem to have taken an interest in Vicki Lane?"

"Vicki?"

"Yeah. I was told some woman around Vicki's age group came to her mother-in-laws place looking for her. I later found out some woman picked Vicki up from the hospital yesterday morning."

"The hospital? What was she doing at the hospital?"

"It's a long story."

"This shit getting kinda' hectic, 'Rise. Maybe we should pull out like 'Bop and Joey? I don't know about you, but um' too young to die? By the way, anybody seen, or heard anything from 'Sweet yet?"

SunRise could see he was beginning to scare Tyrone. "Actually, I have?"

"You did? When? Where she at?"

"Somewhere young Crain and his men can't get to her without meeting opposition. After Vincent dropped her off, Crain's men came after her. Luckily Black-Sun was there."

"So she's safe?"

"So far we all are. I had Black-Sun personally escort her to the safe-house out of state. I apologize for lying about not knowing where she was, but I hate saying more than is necessary. Just my way, you understand?"

"Yeah, a'ight. I feel some type of way about you not sharing that with me. What? All of a sudden you don't trust me?"

"Again, Tye, I apologize. But when a life is at stake, trust will always take a back seat."

"So I guess Robin isn't really on her way out of the country?"

"She's safe."

"Come on 'Rise, man! Ain't none of us safe! And what about that wild card? Didn't you said she move like a spook and fight like a professional killer?"

"We really don't know what she is because we don't know anything about her. Or even if she's in fact a she? What we do know about her is, she saved your life, As far as Vincent is concern, he obviously got greedy once he recognized the names on the disk. He had no idea they would kill to keep their secrete hidden. I don't believe the people who made the disk made it for the Crains, or Teflon Figueroa. It looks more like someone was keeping a close watch on them instead."

Yeah. That kinda' information could send a lot of people to prison?" Tyrone felt the need to point out.

"Are make someone very rich. There is no way they can allow us to live. It doesn't matter whether, or not we had a chance to see what was on it. The mere fact we had it in our possession is enough reason. Which is why they're coming after us so hard. As far as I know, they don't know about the Word file I had Joey delete from the original after making a copy."

"What's in the word file?"

"Information that read like a journal," was all SunRise was willing to tell Tyrone. He knew Tyrone wasn't ready for the truth and he did not want to lie to him anymore. Which was why he neglect mentioning the off-shore account holders Reggy found in the Word file.

"I'm starting to think they had a "pig-in-a-blanket" they didn't know about on their team? I mean, who else would store that kind of information on a single disk. Unless you think something else is going on?"

"If you're right, Tye'. The undercover had to be one of those Dominicans at that house in Regal Park? The same Dominican Crain pushed, remember? Who more than likely already new about us."

"So I'm right?"

"I don't think so. I think the disk was made for the person in the game whose name isn't on it. Which could be our wild-card, or even Henderson's wife?"

"And you don't think it's the feds? Are you sure about all this, 'Rise? I mean, shit sound kinda' far fetched? Did I tell you Crain had a file on me. Maybe we should involve the Feds. 'Cause if you wrong and I'm right, we could be just as guilty as the people who committed the actual murder. But if we come clean now, I bet they can help us. What do you think?"

SunRise looked at Tyrone suspiciously. "I'm surprised you would even ask that, Tye. If it was the feds, they would have pulled the plug and moved in a long time ago. Besides, people like the Crains will never see one day in jail. Prisons were built to protect people like the Crains from people like us. You out of all people should realize that by now."

He gave Tyrone a moment to allow his words to sink in before changing the subject. "Be careful if you intend to talk to Mike's wife again. We both know how close she is to her late husband's financiers. I don't know if I told you, but I also checked her out. Mainly her past. It's questionable. When describing her. The word, siren comes to mind. I never met her, but was told she's the type of woman that could leave you with the impression she had been flirting with you?" SunRise thought of the woman he saw in Cape May Court House going into Rossi's lawyer's office to pick up the package he dropped off for Robin.

"Well... I met her and she didn't leave me with zip. If she had, I didn't notice."

"How she look?" SunRise curiously asked.

"For a white woman? She was fine as hell, but you know me. I like my meat dark."

"And you never got the impression she was trying to come on to you? I was told she could stroke a man's ego with a single glance in passing," he briefly glanced at his watch.

"Hell no," Tyrone said almost defensively. His thoughts drifted to the moment of his meeting with her when he could have swore she glanced at his crotch.

"I have an out of town meeting," SunRise changed the subject while slipping his coat back on.

"How long you gonna be gone?" Tyrone was relieved to be off of the subject of Catherine Henderson. Aside from the fact he couldn't stop thinking about her. He often got the strangest feeling SunRise could read his thoughts, which terrified him.

"As long as it takes," he said, finally looking at Tyrone to ask, "You think it's wise to go see the woman who probably set you up?"

Caught completely off guard, Tyrone didn't know what to say. "Now that you put it that way, I don't know?" He really didn't know if it was wise to see her again. Especially after she set him up. But for the life of him, he just couldn't stop thinking about her. Mostly the way she gazed at him while he was speaking. Truth be told, he really wasn't sure if she had actually  glanced at his crotch?  He wanted to believe she was as big on him as he was on her, but when it came to Catherine Henderson? He couldn't be sure of anything.

"Try to stay alive while I'm gone," SunRise told him while closing the folder. He stood with the folder in one hand and the umbrella in the other. "You should try talking to her on the phone before stepping into the unknown," SunRise suggested before leaving.

Tyrone was about to call Catherine's hotel when his phone began to ring. "Yeah?"

"Tyrone?" asked a woman's voice.

"Yeah. Who's this?" At first, he thought it might be the woman who saved his life last night. But when she spoke a second time, he wasn't so sure.

"Tyrone Sharp?"

"Yeah! Who this?" he yelled with annoyance.

"This is Catherine Henderson. We spoke yesterday in the lobby of my ...."

"I remember," he immediately cut her off. "What's up?" He was surprised to hear from her, yet extremely pleased at the same time. He wanted to scream at her for setting him up with Junior Crain's men, but didn't want to scare her away with accusations. After all, he rationalized, she may have a perfectly good explanation. At least that's what he was hoping.

"Please... call me, Catherine."

"Okay, Catherine. What's up?"

"It's very important that I see you. Can you please come to my hotel. I've already informed the clerk at the desk to send you right up."

"Yesterday when I talked to you, not only did you blow smoke up my ass, you set me up. By the way, how the hell did you get this number? It's unlisted."

"Look, maybe I made a mistake. Sorry to have bothered you, Mr. Sharp. Good-bye!" And just like that, she hung-up. Tyrone felt a pain in the pit of his stomach. Everything he told himself he was not going to do, he did anyway. Blowing the only legitimate reason he had to see her again.

"Oh no you don't. You don't get off that easy," he thought out loud.

Ten minutes later, Tyrone was standing at the front desk of Catherine's hotel. His plan was to try and explain to the clerk that Mrs. Henderson was expecting him. When, immediately after giving his name, the clerk interrupted him.

"Go right up, Mr. Sharp. She's expecting you. Suite 406, fourth floor.

He couldn't believe how easy that was. "Thank you," he said before walking off towards the elevator.

Standing directly in front of suite 406, Tyrone was about to knock when it had occurred to him she might be setting him up again? Instead of knocking, he placed his ear to the door and listened. He thought he had heard something on the other side when all of a sudden, the door opened. Catherine is standing there in her bare feet wearing nothing more than a three quarter inch, satin robe. He got an instance hard-on.

She smiled and said, "I thought I heard someone knock. Come in," she walked over to a wing-back armchair in the living space to sit.

Tyrone slowly stepped into the suite and cautiously looked around. It wasn't until he closed the door behind him before noticing the soft sound of Babyface's, "Soon As I Get Home" playing on a shelf system.

"Have a seat," she motioned with her hand for him to sit in a twin armchair that had been facing hers. "I can't tell you how pleased I am you changed your mind and decided to come."

He looked around the large, extravagant suite some more just to make sure they were alone. He then looked at the identical armchair facing the one she is sitting in. He takes a seat across the room on the sofa instead. He didn't trust himself sitting that close to her. She was gorgeous in a way he couldn't describe. His attraction to her was far from physical. It was on a much different level. After all, she was a skinny white woman. Yet, there was something about her that really turned him on. From her make-up, which was by no means, subtle. To her long golden blond hair and the manner in which it had been styled. Even her long chisel beak-like nose and its' tightly pinched nostrils that were so narrow, he found himself wondering if she was actually able to breathe. Then there were her razor thin, perfectly shaped lips that were naturally cherry-red in color. Her best feature however, were her eyes. Hauntingly beautiful in a Meg Foster sort of way, they were a light grayish-blue in color and seem to have the power to captivate most men who were foolish enough to gaze into them.

"You said something about needing to see me?"

"I heard what happen to you last night. If I knew you were going to pry, I would have warned you beforehand," she said, doing a complete three-sixty.

Visibly surprised, he couldn't believe the position she was now taking. "Mrs. Henderson, are you serious?"

"I'm very serious, Mr. Sharp. And please, call me Catherine," she reminded him.

"Look, Catherine. I don't know what kinda' game you playing, but I ain't the one. I came to you yesterday out of pure concern for your safety. First, you lied to me. Then had the nerve to point me out to Crain's bulls."

Her face tightened. It was obvious she didn't appreciate not being taken serious, but managed to maintain her composure. "Mr. Sharp," she began. "when you came to see me yesterday. I had no idea you were mixed up with Johnathen. I called you over here to apologize and make sure you were all right?"

"I fine, no thanks to you. And for your information, I ain't mixed up with your boy, Crain. Hell, yesterday was the first time I ever saw him."

She stood, walked over and sat on the sofa next to him. Tyrone couldn't help noticing her body-language as she took his hand and held it in hers. She felt so warm and soft, he began to feel self-conscious and secretly prayed his hand did not feel clammy in hers.

"If you're talking about Johnathen's security? They were actually asking me who you were? I really didn't think much of it at the time until I told them your name. When I saw them go after you, I sent Asmar to throw them off. I guess it didn't work?" she said, staring at the Band-Aid on the side of his face. She was still holding his hand when she lightly touched the band-aid with her other hand. He backed away from her touch, startling her. She looked at him, "I'm sorry. Does it hurt much?" she asked. Her eyes were like vampire fangs. Sucking what little will-power he had left out of him. He wasn't sure what to think. The story she just told him about sending Asmar to throw them off made perfect sense.

"Actually, it doesn't hurt at all. It's nothing. Just a small cut, that's all."

"Mr. Sharp, please stay away from those men. They're very bad people who don't play around."

"It's okay, Catherine. You can call me, Tyrone. You're starting to make me feel kinda' old tagging me with that 'Mister' title." She gazed into his eyes. He felt himself getting weak and forced a nervous laugh that did not go over too well. "I intend to stay away from the likes of Crain and his suits. What I'd like to know from you is, why the sudden concern for my welfare? We just met yesterday?"

She smiled that smile of hers and flashed her long lashes at him. "He's not my boyfriend, or man for that matter. Johnathen, I mean. If you're wondering, the answer is, no. I am not seeing him. I just work for him, that's all. Oh, sure, he's been very good to me, but my feeling for someone can't be bought like some dime store hooker. You know what um' saying?" she did another three-sixty and went straight 'hood on him. Tyrone almost got lost in her gaze as she stared into his eyes as if she was waiting for him to make the first move.

"I hear you," he said for a lack of anything clever to say. He briefly glanced at his watch then stood.

She released his hand and stood with him. They were close now and he found himself paralyzed by the woman who stood a foot from him. He tried to walk away, but his legs refuse to move.

"You're not leaving, are you?" she asked. Her voice took on another tone, soft and suggestive.

He wanted to say, I'll never leave you. Then drop to his knees and eat her out. He thought about SunRise and Renee's warnings about her. "Unless you have something else to say, I don't see any reason why I should stay?" He didn't know where that came from, but he was proud of himself for finding the strength to resist her.

"I think you know why, Tyrone." She moved closer and their bodies touched. Tyrone felt himself getting weak and excited at the same time. As she stood staring into his eye as if she was studying them. He got a good whiff of her scent and found it overwhelmingly sweet and seductive. "I've always been a very good judge of character," she continued. "Especially when I meet someone and the attraction is mutual."

Without taking her eyes off of him, she rubbed his crotch and he almost busted off right then and there. She smiled, took his hand in hers and guided it between her thighs. She was wet between her legs and on fire. She brought his fingers to her lip and sucked on them. She then kissed him lightly on the lips while slipping off his coat. As he stood there in a trance, she slid her tongue between his lips. She taste delicious and he wanted nothing more than to gobble her up. But a voice in his head kept screaming at him to leave before it was too late.

He visualized SunRise for strength and it appeared to be working. A wave of guilt swept over him. Just as he found the straight to  leave, she dropped to her knees and began fumbling with his 'fly'. He opened his mouth to protest, but no words came out. He grabbed her hands to stop her while thinking about Angela Davis, Assata Shakur and countless other strong black women he had often envisioned himself settling down with. And for a moment, he actually thought he found the strength to resist her. Until she looked up at him with those eyes of hers. He felt himself getting weak again and released her hands.  He knew he was going to regret it, but no longer cared. As she continued to fumble with his fly, he wasted no time slipping out of his sweater before removing the vest, his guns, then t-shirt. She slid down his pants and underwear. Once she had his hefty nine inches free from its constrains. She proceeded  to work her magic on him while fingering herself. When she felt his legs beginning to buckle, she knew she had him.

# CHAPTER 10

When Vicki returned to the suite later that day, Camille had not yet returned. Feeling alone and somewhat bored, she sat in the sitting area by the window flipping through the pages of an old fashion magazine. She couldn't remember the last time she actually had an opportunity to sit back and just relax. She not only found it nice, but therapeutic as well.

As she continued flipping through the pages. She stopped when she saw a young urban model who bore a striking resemblance to Londell, her late husband. A sadness came over her. She turned the page and tried to focus on something else, but it didn't work. Each page seem to reflect a memory of him. She tried remembering his laugh, but couldn't. Probably because he rarely ever did. She needed to remember that about him and wish she could remember more of him. More things they did together besides killing people. At least she would have that. A firm memory of his smile, his laughter, his love, but there was so little of him in her memory left. Camille had told her it was for the best that she leave the past behind and look ahead.

"What's up?"

Vicki jumped and turned to see Camille standing in back of her. "Camille!" she snapped. "You scared the shit outta' me."

Camille slipped out of her coat and tossed it on the bed. "Sorry. I didn't mean to startle you. What you doing?" she asked again while sitting on the bed to remove her boots

"Just thinking, that's all."

"About what?"

"Nothing in particular. Just things," Vicki told her while still flipping through the pages.

Camille walked over to the bed and sat. "If I'd been on the job, you'd be dead," she pointed out while proceeding to remove her boots.

Still flipping through the pages of the magazine, Vicki simply replied, "Yeah... whatever."

Camille could see Vicki was either bored, or depressed and beginning to lose interest in her. Which seemed to stem from a direct result of the trip she took to her late mother-in-law's apartment. "You eat anything yet?"

Vicki sat the magazine down and walked over to help Camille with her boots. "The landlady at my mother-in-law's gave me dinner. She said some white woman fitting your description came around to see me right after I went to the hospital?"

Camille lifted her left leg so Vicki could remove her boot." That was me," she said. "I told you I came to see you, but the landlady told me I just missed you."

"I remember," said Vicki. Once she had the first boot off, Camille lifted her right leg. "She also told me SunRise was there looking for me." Vicki tugged at the heel of Camille's boot until she finally slid it off.

"SunRise?"

Vicki stood and sat on the bed next to her. "He's the guy I thought sent you to pick me up. The one who placed the contract on Michael Henderson."

"What was his beef with, Henderson?"

"The same beef he has with anyone who sell drugs. It's a long story. Anyway, Ms. Stella wanted me to stay with her. I told her I was staying with a friend."

"What about the funeral? You find out when they gonna' have it?"

"Yeah, but I don't think I'm going. I can't see her like that again. I explained to her how I felt and I think she understood. She asked me what I wanted to do about all Ma' things. I told her to give everything to charity and my husband's car and the family photos to Mr. Willie. He's a friend of the family."

"That was nice of you," Camille said before changing the subject. "You wanna finish hearing about my past?"

"Are you going to finish it this time and not leave me hanging like you did the last time? 'Cause if you're not...."

"I'll finish."

"Promise?" Vicki got comfortable on the bed.

"I promise," said Camille, laying down beside Vicki before beginning. "I told you Frenchie, my mom was murdered, right?"

"Yeah. I'm sorry to hear...."

"I never told you how," Camille quickly cut her off.

"Or what happen to you after she died?" Vicki reminded her.

"Yeah. After Frenchie became too sick to work the street. She came up with the bright idea to rent me out for sexual favors. I was only nine, or ten at the time. It happened one hot ass summer afternoon back in '82, if I'm not mistaken. After I've been dragged around from one rat hole to the next. Frenchie finally found the opportunity she had been waiting for. An opportunity that came in the form of a greedy, heartless, street level drug dealer name, Red. For Red, it wasn't the first time an addict tried to pass off their child just to get high. Normally, he would have never went for some shit like that. But as soon as that ass-hole saw me, he was all over it. The fact that I was this skinny-ass kid didn't seem to mean shit. Something about me must have told him there was a financial gain in it for him. Because that ass-hole didn't hesitate to make the deal. A few minutes after Frenchie shot-up, she was dead. An hour after she died, Red sold me to some flamboyant, forty year old pig of a pimp name, Mink. Who, by the way, had no intentions of waiting until I became of age. Like Red, Mink wasn't into children either. His plan was to pimp me out to his special clients. Men who paid him big money to have sex with children behind closed doors. But first, he had to turn me out. An unwilling participant was very bad for business.

"Turn you out?"

"Yeah. Make me a willing participant."

"As if that mattered. You were under age! A child!" Vicki found herself getting emotional.

"As if he cared. He gave his bottom bitch, Angelica two weeks to turn me. Angelica, Angel for short, was this Greek bitch in her mid to late thirties at the time. She had been with Mink during his entire career as a pimp."

"I know I shouldn't be asking this, but how did she look?" Vicki asked only to put a face on the person in Camille's story.

"Angel was a short, petite bitch. She wasn't what you consider pretty, but she was a sexy lil' thing with large, light brown eyes. Her best feature was her full lips and long, straight, jet black hair that extended to the small of her back. She also had this long, thick-ass tongue that did strange things to me. But that's another story. The bitch was a beast when it came to turning woman out for Mink, and a child was by no means an exception. Angel's plan was to turn me out on sex like Frenchie had been turned out on drugs. A week had past and I still haven't been introduced to sex yet. They brought me nice clothes. I ate well and got to live in this big house with Cat and four other women who treated me like family.

149

"Who the hell is Cat?"

"At the time, she was one of Mink's girls and the only one who appeared to really care about me. She had been with Mink and Angel for awhile and told me she knew Frenchie before I was born. Her clients use to call her Mystique because that's what she gave them, mystery. Mink would come up to the house at least twice a day, but never stayed long. Most of the time it was either to pick up the other three girls late at night, or drop them off early in the morning. Sometimes, one or two of the girls wouldn't return for days. When they finally did, they would look worn out. Like they been running the track for weeks. Two weeks had passed and Angel had explained all there was to know about the male and female's anatomy. We smoked weed, sipped some of the best wines, and watched porn all night while Angel molested me. It wasn't long before I began looking forward to her abuse. God help me but to this day, I still think about the way she made me feel." Camille's eyes became glazed with a perverted lust as she remembered. "I have to hand it to her, though. The bitch was good."

Vicki frowned at the thought of what they did to Camille. She thought of the perverse pleasures Camille had introduced her to and began feeling guilty. She thought about the three year old little girl named, Kiki who use to live across the hall with her mother. And like Camille, she too had been molested by someone she knew and trusted. But unlike Camille's situation, Kiki's mother caught her boyfriend before he was able to do any real damage.

"One night," Camille went on to say. "Mink came to the house with a well dressed elderly white man. When Mink called Angel down stairs into the front room. I ease-dropped and over heard them talking about me. "This here is Mr. Crain, a valued client of ours," he told her.

"Nice to meet you, Mr. Crain," Angel said with a fake smile.

Crain smiled politely and said, "The pleasure is all mine," while taking her hand in his before kissing it. Angel giggled like some silly-ass school-girl who found herself in the presence of royalty.

Mink smiled and said, "I was telling Mr. Crain about our new find, Camille. Is she ready?"

I remember him sounding kinda' worried when he asked her.

"Have I ever let you down, daddy?" Angel asked proudly. I couldn't see them, but I just know that bitch was smiling. Mink's premature concerns turned into a huge verbal pat on her freaky ass.

"That's my girl," he said, "Show Mr. Crain to her room," he ordered.

Angel quickly grabbed his old, perverted ass by the hand and lead him up stairs to the bed-room she and I shared together. I was sitting on the edge of the large bed when they stepped into the room. "Camille," she began. "This is a very special friend of ours. Mink and I want you to treat him real nice, you hear?" Without waiting for a reply, she exited the room. Leaving me alone with that old, freaky bastard. I was just a baby. Confused and scared to death. Especially when he slowly approach me with this sinister smile." She paused for a moment and shook as if she had just felt a chill. "Shit gave me the creeps," she said while remembering. "When he sat on the edge of the bed next to me, I shivered. He noticed and began to stroke the side of my face with the back of his old-ass-hand.

"They weren't exaggerating about you." He said, tossing his suit jacket over the arm of a chair next to the vanity mirror. I remember as if it was yesterday. "Come here," he said. When I didn't move. He grabbed me by the wrist and guided me directly in front of him. Standing there in my brand new navy-blue, Catholic-school uniform, I was terrified. I held my head down looking at my black, patent-leathers shoes and white bob socks. He gently lifted my head by the chin with an index finger, forcing me to look up at him. "My god, you are such a beautiful little girl," he repeated to himself.

"Thank you," I heard myself saying in an effort to be polite while trying to avoid making eye contact. I could still feel his eyes undressing me and the shit made me feel real uncomfortable. Angel had parted my long, dyed, sandy-blond hair down the middle of my head and styled it in long pig-tails.

"Do you mind if I undress you?" he asked. I was too young to even know how to answer that. So I just shrugged and watched while he slowly lifted my head so I would look up at him. He stood, lifted my new dress over my head and arms. Then flung it over his shoulder without taking his eyes off of me. I couldn't believe he would treat my new dress like that. My mouth dropped with shock while my eyes followed the dress as it flew across the room until finally landing on the floor. I wanted to run and get it, but he lifted me up and placed me in the middle of the bed. After removing my shoes and socks. He began to take off his clothes. I was scared to death sitting there on the bed wearing nothing but a pair of white cotton panties. I remember him removing the last of his clothing, but for the life of me, I can't remember anything else that happened after that. Except maybe dreading what was coming next."

"Isn't that the man you asked me about when we first met?" Vicki interrupted to ask.

"Yes and no," Camille said before continuing. "Two years had passed since that first encounter with my first John. And still, I never really got use to what was required of me from Mink's special clients. Cat really helped me get through it all."

"How?"

"By teaching me how to blank out my encounters with the johns. Unlike the others, I think she actually cared about me. Back then, she had to be about seventeen, or eighteen years older than me. I remember telling her I wanted to die because I had no intentions of staying a slave for the rest of my life. She grabbed me by my arms and shook me until she had my full attention.

"Now you listen to me, young lady. I don't ever wanna' hear you talk like that again. YOU HEAR ME! PROMISE ME!" she was highly upset with me. Shouting at me like she done lost her damn mind. After I promised. She made me a promise. She told me she had a client who was negotiating a deal to buy her contract and promised to come back for me."

"Did she?" Vicki couldn't help asking.

Without answering, Camille continued. "Exactly one week later, I was up-stairs in my room entertaining one of Mink's special clients when we heard a lot of commotion going on down stairs. I was about to go check it out when the client grabbed a fist full of my hair an said, "Don't stop, little girl. I'm almost there," while forcing my head back down on his lil' ass knob. As soon as I went back down on him someone kicked open my bedroom door. Scared the shit out of me. I jumped to my feet while wiping my mouth with the back of my hand."

"Yuck!" Vicki found herself verbally reacting to the disgusting mental image Camille just painted.

"When I saw those two gun-men rush into the room. I ran to the corner and crouched on the floor. The two men ignored me and started pistol-whipping my client. Scared me so much, I closed my eyes and covered my ears. I heard a muffled gun-shot sound. Then it got quiet. I didn't want to open my eyes, but curiosity got the better of me and I peeked. When I saw this tall shadow heading towards me, I just knew I was next. The moment I felt this hand trying to grab me. I screamed and tried to crawl away. He quickly grabbed me by the arm and violently dragged me out of the corner. When he placed a gun to my head, the other gunman asked, "What the hell you doing?" while going through the dead client's pant.

"Fuck it look like? You heard what Jay said, fool. NO WITNESSES!" the tall man shouted at him.

"She ain't no witness. She's a kid. We don't do chil'ren, remember?"

"Only if the child is deaf, dumb and blind. Other than that, it's a rap." He was about to pull the trigger when the other man rushed over and placed a gun to his head.

"Yo, my man, you hard of hearing?"

"MAN! IS YOU CRAZY!" the tall man shouted. Even though he still had his gun to my head, I could tell he was scared to death. Now he knew how I felt with his gun to my head, but I doubt if it ever crossed his mind.

"I said, NO!" the other man shouted at him.

"Man, you don't call no shots!"

With his gun still to the tall man's head. The other man said, "I just did!"

The tall man slowly removed his gun from my head and released the tight grip he had around my upper arm. "A'ight, Maz'. You got that. But just remember when Jay ask, you found her."

"Just take your skinny, fraudulent ass down the hall somewhere. I got this."

The tall man shot the man he referred to as, Maz' a 'twenty-five-to-life' gaze and mumbled under his breath, "Punk mu'fucka'," before leaving the room.

"WHAT!" Maz' shouted behind him, but the tall man had already left the room. "Yeah, that's what I thought!" Something told me it wasn't gonna' be over between the two men until one of them were dead.

Within minutes after the tall man left the room, there were more gun shots, "POP! POP! POP!" I was still on the floor when Maz' looked at me and asked, "How old is you?" I must have been in shock, or something because I wanted to answer, but couldn't. "Look, lil' girl," he said. " Right now, um' the only friend you got. Ma' man down stairs don't like leaving any witnesses, you dig what um' saying? Now... umma' ask you one more time. How old is you?"

"I'll be eleven next month."

"What's your name and where's your family?"

I told him my name was, Camille. "I don't know where Frenchie is. She left me with some man who brought me to this house two years ago."

"Who's Frenchie?"

"I told him my mom. He asked for my last name.

"LaRue," I told him.  He looked at me as if he had just seen a ghost. "Frenchie LaRue! You  mean to tell me you that lil' girl Frenchie use to  drag with her everywhere she went? Well I'll be damned." His expression softened as if he was now seeing me for the first time. "Frenchie was your mom," he repeated to himself. I just shook my head up and down. It never even dawned on me that he had spoke about her in the past tense.

"She left me with some man. When she didn't come get me, he brought me here." I told him again in case he hadn't heard me the first time. He grabbed me by the arm and pulled me to my feet.

"Come on," he said, literally dragging me from the room. As soon as we got down stairs, I saw Angel and Mink. They were both tied-up in separate chairs in the dining room. I didn't see the other three women who worked out of the house. I guess they got the three pops I heard up stairs. I remember being glad Cat wasn't there at the time because if she would have been, they probably would have murdered her, too. Mink had been beaten real bad and was out cold. His face was swollen and bleeding badly. Angel, on the other hand, was crying and pleading for her life.

"Please! Please! Please, don't hurt me. I'm just a whore. I don't know anything. I swear!"

It was by far her best performance yet. But this short, light-skinned, muscle bound guy sporting a clean shaven head wasn't going for it. I couldn't see his face, but assumed he was Jay, the one who didn't like leaving witnesses. The tall man who tried to push my wig back up stairs stood next to him. He also had his back to me. His gun on the other hand, which was inches from Angel's head, was something I will never forget. For a moment, I actually thought I was gonna' be a'ight until Maz' told the guy who was running shit, "Dig, man. I found Frenchie's kid up stairs?" My heart sunk to my feet. I looked up at my so-called savior and remember thinking, This fool must be tripping. He gon' get me killed! The guy running shit finally turned to face me. As soon as I saw his face, my heart skipped another beat. He stared at me with piercing, cold eyes and uttered, "Cami?" in the form of a question, but never changed expressions. I didn't answer. I was too afraid to say anything."

"Oh, shit!" Vicki shouted excitedly.

"The tall man Looked at Jaedm, then me. Then back at Jaedm and asked, "You know her, Jay?" without taking his gun from Angel's head. Still staring at me, Jaedm never answered the tall man. Instead, he slowly produced a silencer and attached it to his nine-millimeter.

"She's only ten, man," Maz' quickly pointed out.

Without taking his eyes off of me, he just said, "I know." Then turned to face Angel and Mink again. As he raised the gun to Mink's head. Maz' pulled me close to him and covered my eyes with his hand just before Jaedm pulled the trigger. I managed to still see everything. Angel, didn't. But as soon as she realized Mink's blood, bone fragments and brain matter had plastered on the side of her face, hair and blouse, she became hysterical. Almost lost her mind. Screamed so load, Jaedm had to viciously smacked her in the mouth with the bud of his gun just to shut her up. He then detached the silencer, wiped the gun clean and placed it in Mink's hand. When he turned to face me again. Maz' quickly snatched his hand from my eyes as if he didn't want Jaedm to know he had speared me the sight of such a gruesome act. He looked at Maz' first, then at me. "Shoot that bitch, Lil-Nigga',"

158

he ordered the tall man without taking his eyes off of me. I stared back without so much as a blink. My eyes began to fill with tears and I couldn't stop my lips from quivering. Not from sorrow. It was anger that drove me to tears. I remembered thinking, "Fuck you, muthafucka! You want me dead? You do it, you bitch-ass-muthafucka'!" As soon as Lil-Nigga' blew Angel's brains out. I realized Jaedm wasn't referring to me when he told Lil' Nigga to, "shoot that bitch". He and I had been staring each other down. And because I never flinched when the gun went off, or took my eyes off of him, I could tell he was impressed, but tried not to showed it.

"Then how'd you know he was impressed?" Vicki asked.

"He smiled. Not with his lips, with his eyes. I ain't gonna' lie. I was fuckin' paralyzed. I just knew he was talking about shooting me. Just as we were about to leave? That bitch-ass tall guy said, "What about the kid?"

Jaedm abruptly stopped and asked, "What about her?" He was so cool, he never even bothered to turn and face the man who just questioned him.

"She gotta' go, too!" the man complained. I got the impression that he had pissed Jaedm off. Because when he finally did turn around to face, Lil-Nigga'. His face was tight-as-hell. I guess Lil-Nigga' never notice, because when Jaedm asked for his gun, he smiled arrogantly at me while handing Jaedm his gun. I smiled back, then watched as Jaedm briefly examined the weapon, cocked it and shot the tall man between the eyes at point-blank range. Once again, he wipe the gun clean and placed it in the right hand of the man he had just murdered.

"That shit ain't gonna' work, Jaedm. You making it seem like they all shot themselves?" Maz', the man who stopped Lil' Nigga' from shooting me, felt the need to point out.

Jaedm laughed. "I know," he said. "I just wanna' fuck with, homicide. Let 'em try to figure this one out."

Just before the three of us left the house, he pulled a pack of cigarettes from his pocket and tapped the pack against the side of his index finger. As soon as a cigarette slid halfway out of the pack. He pulled it all the way out with his lips. Then looked at Maz', who just walked off into the kitchen. When Maz' returned, Jaedm asked him for a light. Maz' checked his coat pocket first. Then found a book of matches in his pant pocket. I watched as he removed a single match from the book and struck it lit. He then carefully held the lit match under Jaedm's cigarette. After Jaedm lit his cigarette, he removed a pair of black leather gloves from his coat pocket and slide them on while peering down at me. I stared back. He took a long pull off of his cigarette, then plucked it into the kitchen. "Let's roll," he said, leading the way out of the house. Maz' and I followed. I thought about the cigarette he had just lit and remembered wondering why he only took one pull before discarding it?

While we were driving down the street, there was a huge explosion that shook the entire block. Jaedm and I looked at one another. I later found out he had been secretly keeping taps on me and Frenchie.

Actually, I think he was surprised Frenchie lasted as long as she had. When Frenchie died from an overdose. No one claimed the body. Jaedm stepped up and saw to it she received a proper burial. He had just assumed I was staying with my grandparents until he found me at Mink's house. Turns out, it was Cat who put the contract out on Mink and his girls."

"The girl you attached yourself to, right?" Vicki asked just to make sure.

"Yeah. Cat' hired Jaedm to get rid of Mink and his girls. She wanted out of the business and didn't want her pass to catch up with her later."

"That was kinda' drastic don't you think? She almost got you killed?"

"I guess I was the exception. I never really thought she was serious about coming back for me. Guess I was wrong. At the age of nine, I was  molested and raped, but I learned to deal with it. No matter how sick and twisted the experience, it's always your first that sticks with you. Mink's biggest clientele was Johnathen Crain. I later found out he was a powerful New York businessman who had his hands in the pockets of a lot of important people who were stupid enough to patronize southern illegal brothel."

"You want to make him pay for raping you?"

"He's old now. Still, he have to be held accountable."

"What ever happened to Jaedm?"

"When Jaedm killed Mink. The locals somehow found out about it?"

"What happened after the three of you left Mink's house?"

"After we left Mink's house. Maz' drove while Jaedm and I sat in the back. I guess I changed a lot from what he remembered about me because he kept staring. Physically, I definitely changed. Probably in ways he couldn't get over. He probably remembered a skinny little kid starving for food and the attention of her mother. I was now taller and had the body of a sixteen year old. Mentally, I was distant, apathetic and broken. I remember him asking, "You know who I am?" I did, but shook my head to indicate that I didn't. "Good answer," he said while smiling at Mazeroti."

"Who the hell is Mazeroti?" Vicki quickly asked.

"That's Maz'. His name is Mazeroti, but we called him Maz' for short. Jaedm," Camille went on to say, "had the nerve to ask me, "You wanna' know why I killed your friends?" I was afraid to answer. I held my head down looking nervously at my hands which were resting in my lap. "Because someone paid me to. I didn't know you'd be there. If I had known, I woulda' murdered 'em for free, you dig." He pause for a moment before continuing. "They weren't your friends, Cami. They were bad people who used nice little girls like you to line their pockets with silly shit." He pause again as if he wanted to tell me, or ask me something but couldn't find the words. Finally he asked, "What happen to you, Cami? How the hell did you end up at that house with those people?"

I still had no idea my mom was dead, so I told him the same thing I told Maz'. "Frenchie left me with some man who brought me to

Mink's house two years ago. The next day, Angel told me they found Frenchie dead from an overdose. I didn't have nowhere else to go. Angel told me that Mink would take care of me as long as I took care of his friends. I never believed what she said about Frenchie being dead, though. I just pretended because I wanted to stay there with Cat. She was real nice to me." Jaedm face twisted with a indigestible mixture of anger and confusion.

"You been living at that brothel since Frenchie died?"

I looked at him in disbelief. "Frenchie really dead? Angel was telling the truth?" I asked, hoping it wasn't true. When Jaedm didn't say anything, I realized it was true.

As the three of us drove in silence. I was suddenly confronted with the realization that I was all alone. I felt sick to my stomach and wanted to cry, but couldn't.

"Um' sorry about Frenchie, Cami," Jaedm finally broke the silence. "If it helps to know," he continued. "I made sure she got a proper burial. If you want, I'll have Maz' drive by the cemetery so you can pay your respects?"

Lost in my own thoughts, I never really heard a word he said. I was too busy thinking about the man who had given my mother the poison that ended her life. I hated him and couldn't stop visualizing the grin on his face when Frenchie offered me to him.

"Look here," Jaedm began. "if you worried about having some place to crash. Don't," he assured me. "I have a friend who'll take good care of you."

My only thoughts were getting the piece-of-shit who murdered my mom. I started crying. "That man killed Frenchie," I finally spoke as tears began to storm down my face.

"What man?" he quickly asked.

"That man," I shouted, "who gave Frenchie that dope!" I was angry and wanted them to know I was angry.

Jaedm looked up front at Maz', who had been watching through the rear-view. He then looked at me again and asked, "You 'member his name, or how he look? Anything at all? 'Cause I'll handle it. If that's what you want, you dig?""

"I remember Frenchie calling him, Red. He had a greedy grin, too."

Jaedm looked at Maz' and asked, "What the hell is a, greedy grin? You know who the fuck she takin' 'bout, Maz'?"

"I know exactly who she talkin' 'bout. I had a beef with him and his boys back in the early seventies."

"You sure y'all talkin' 'bout the same chump?"

"Sounds like 'em. The only lame I know with a greasy grin named, Red, you know."

164

Jaedm became silent. I thought he was formulating a plan. He then looked at me, but didn't say anything.

"Only one way to find out," said Maz'. He looked at Jaedm in the rear-view and asked, "You want me to swing through 'Middle Town' and try to find him? Just to be sure, you know. Cami can point him out, you know." When Jaedm declined. I was hurt and felt betrayed. Mainly because I didn't think he cared.

We drove for what seemed like hours, but in actuality it was more like forty-five minutes before Maz' finally parked on a quiet, middle-class residential street. While Jaedm quickly got out, Maz' and I wait in the car.

"I'll be right back," he assured before leaving. Maz' and I watched him run across the street to a small house. As soon as he went inside, I took the liberty to ask Maz' something that had been bothering me about Jaedm?

"Why he shoot that man? I thought y'all was friends?"

Maz' turned in his seat to look at me. Because it was the first time I had ever initiate conversation. He not only welcomed the question, but also saw it as the perfect opportunity to ask me a few of his own. "What?" he asked, making sure he had heard me right.

"Why he shoot that man at Mink's house? He just shot him in the face like it was nothing. I thought y'all was friends?"

Maz' smiled coldly. "Because, Lil-Nigga' questioned him. Jaedm knew he either had to murder you, or him. He chose his own over you. Now let me ask you something. Why would he do that? Choose you over his own, and don't lie to me. Remember, um' the same cat who stopped Lil-Nigga' from shootin' you, see what 'um sayin'?"

"I remember. Thank you," I said while nervously glancing at the house Jaedm had disappeared into.

"Well?" Maz' impatiently waited for an answer.

I hesitated. I wasn't sure if it was wise to speak of Jaedm behind his back. Nor did I want to anger Maz' by not answering his question. "M-m-maybe I shouldn't talk about him behind his back. He might get mad. Ain't you scared he'll get mad and shoot you, too?"

Mazeroti's expression turned cold and hard. "We all gotta' die some day," he replied.

"Then maybe you should ask him when he gets back." I flatly replied.

He burst out laughing, then turned back around in his seat and lit a cigarette. "I see why Jaedm likes you," he said to no one in particular. "You crazy than-a-muthafucka," I wasn't sure if I should thank him, or just keep my mouth shut. Ultimately I chose the latter. It was obvious the less I said, or pretended not to know, the better off I was around both men." Camille then stood and walked off into the bathroom, closing the door behind her.

# CHAPTER 11

The moment Camille finally came out of the bathroom, Vicki immediately asked. "What happen when Jaedm got back?"

"When Jaedm got back, he signaled Maz' out of the car. They walked a few feet away from the car and began talking. I couldn't hear what they were saying. I just assumed it had something to do with me. When they returned to the car, Maz' got in behind the wheel and Jaedm asked me to step out. I got out and walked with him towards the house he'd just came out of. As we walked, he told me he made arrangements for me to stay with a close friend of his.

"She lives alone and can protect you if something should jump off. You okay with that?" he asked as if I had some say in the matter. When I shrugged, he became angry and shouted, "I asked you a question and I never repeat myself!"

"I trust you," I quickly replied. I wasn't sure if it was the answer he was looking for. I just said what I felt.

His expression changed from anger to confusion. "You trust me. Lil' girl, you don't even know me."

"You don't know me, but you trust me to keep my mouth shut?" I quickly said. Again, without thinking.

He stared down at me. Right then, I knew I fucked up by speaking too soon. But when he smiled that crooked smile of his. I smiled with him and felt a little more at ease. "Good point."

Before we reached the house. I remember seeing a small dark figure standing in front of the house, waiting. As we got closer. That dark figure turned out to be a woman."

Vicki immediate asked, "Who was she?"

"Jaedm introduced her to me as, Ms. Patti," Camille said while sitting on the bed again.

"Jaedm ever come back for you?" Vicki curiously asked.

"That was the last time I ever saw Jaedm again. When he told me Patti was gonna' take care of me. I shoulda' known he wasn't coming back."

"Did she? Take care of you?" Vicki interrupted.

"Absolutely."

"What about Jaedm? She ever tell you what happen to him?"

"No, and I never asked. I stayed with her for four years until she had to leave and couldn't afford to take me with her. For the most part, I ended up on my own. That's when I found out Jaedm had gotten 'bagged' for Mink and his girls murder. I heard Mazeroti was murdered by the police for trying to push an eye-witness. I never found out who the eye witness was, or even if there actually was an eye-witness because no one ever testified. Yet, Jaedm is sitting in prison somewhere and Maz' is still dead."

"You think they actually had a witness?"

"If they did? I've always had my suspicions who it might have been?"

"Who?" asked Vicki.

"The guy who murdered my mother and sold me into slavery."

"You ever get with him?"

"No."

"You never said what happen to, Cat?"

"I didn't see her again until recently. I thought she was gonna' have a stroke when she first realized who I actually was. We had lunch and talked. That's when I learned about Junior, Johnathen Crain's only son. He was the client who secretly bright her contract from Mink. His father never know anything about his son's infatuation with one of the whores from, 'House of a Thousand Minks'. She told me she put herself through school. Then came up here and got married."

"Really? They must have been in love?" Vicki noted.

"I'm sure he was. She, on the other hand, never had any real feelings for him, or any other man as far as I know. She saw him as a way for her to start over."

"They still married?" Vicki asked.

"Not anymore. Her husband is dead."

Vicki looked confused. "I don't understand?"

"She didn't marry Junior. She married someone else."

"Can I ask you something?"

"Of course.

"You promise to be honest with me?"

Camille hesitated before promising to be honest with Vicki.

"Why the sudden interest in me?"

"I think you're special, but not in the way you think I mean. I just think you have a lot of potential to become one of the best in the field. I like to be the one to take you there?"

"Take me where"

"The same place Patti Johnson took me. To the summit of the murder game. The people I'm tracking are tracking your friends, but they don't know about you."

"What people?"

"Junior Crain. The man who pushed Henderson and your husband, then tried to push you. But before you answer, I want you to really think about it. I can't have you going off half cocked thinking you gonna' get some get-back. Revenge is like indulging a thirst that can never be quenched. Eventually you'll end up drowning in a sea of bitterness." Camille cleared her throat before continuing. "Junior made a mistake by ordering the hit on Henderson. He accused Mike of leaking information about the shipment in Queens and had him murdered the very next day.

Because I was already in place, Cat recommended to Junior a female to neutralize the target. I was contacted by one of Junior's handlers; a man name, Bobby White. He was the one who actually contracted me to clear the way to Mike's demise. They needed someone Mike trusted, namely me. While one of their people, namely Spurlock, took him out. Once Spurlock took Henderson out, he was suppose to push me. It didn't work out that way, though. The only people who can actually identify me are you, Cat, Bobby White, and Spurlock. White and Spurlock are now dead. And as far as they know, Cat never actually saw, or met me. The men junior now has working for him are professionals. Trained by the U.S. military."

"Mercenaries?"

"Very good. When Junior hired me, he had no idea he was actually hiring the woman his perverted father use to rape and molest as a child. In this game, Vicki, our lives depend on being who and what we claim to be. I don't mean just looking the part. I'm talking about being able to blend into your environment with ease. Understand?"

"I guess."

"I don't want to pressure you, or anything, but if you plan on getting down with me? I need to know right now."

Not quite sure what was expected of her, Vicki stared at Camille for a moment. Then held her head down in deep thought. She thought about her husband and mother-in-law. She thought about the night she dreamt of having a conversation with Ma'Matty. It was the same night Ma' had peacefully past in her sleep. She could still remember Ma's words as if it had all happened moments ago. Your purpose will find you, Ma' had told her. She looked at Camille again and asked, "What do I have to do?"

Camille smiled and began schooling Vicki on a few things. "I was trained by one of the most ruthless killers of the twenty first century. Not just how to kill, but how to think. There are two limits of human performance; one is a lack of preparation, the other is fear. So far," Camille went on to explain, "you and your partner were just a couple of contract killers. Anyone is capable of that, but to become an assassin there are rules. To become a professional, the riffle is the first thing you learn to use because it allows you to keep your distance. Always wait for the prime shot. The knife is the last because the closer you get to your target, the closer you are in becoming a professional assassin and not before.

The men Crain has working for him are all special forces, former navy seal." Camille headed towards the closet where she retrieved a cream colored leather briefcase and sat it on the bed.

"What's this?" Vicki asked.

Camille opened it and pulled out a folder. "Homework," she said, handing the folder to Vicki. "The man in the file I just hand you heads Junior's team of security. He might not seem like much, but he's good. Getting to Junior is gonna' be difficult because we have to go through him and his men."

Vicki looked at her strangely and asked, "How the hell did you get this information on these people?"

"That's not important right now, but I will eventually teach you to do the same. Ross and his men are trained killers who study their targets. You have to learn how to do the same. It's call research." She paused briefly before adding, "If you fail to plan, your plan will fail."

That night, Camille taught Vicki how to compile an intelligence file on targets and where to look for the information. Explaining, "If you're not satisfied with the intel' on a target, dig deeper." She illustrated how important it was to have good information about what, or who you are dealing with.

"Always use good equipment," she explained. "The kind you can rely on and trust to work every time. Personally, I prefer a rifle for snipping."

Camille took her time teaching Vicki everything she knew. "You have to start getting use to stress. Never get distracted and try not to fuck with caffeine, the last thing you want is the shakes while going for the prime shot."

The next day, Camille trained Vicki how to shoot from a distance and punished her for missing shots. Camille always placed a time limit on Vicki's training. "Your job..." Camille went on to school her, "... may also mean watching. You never know how long you gonna' be observing a target. So make sure you're comfortable because if you're not, your focus will be more on how uncomfortable you are than the mission." As the two women almost pulled an all-nighter. They slept the following day until noon.

Later that evening, they went shopping for a more sophisticated look for Vicki. "The people we're going after," Camille explained, "ain't from the 'hood. More like gated communities and educated in the best schools. In order to even get close to them, you have to appear to be from the same class."

"Why?" Vicki whined.

"Because your life will depend on it," Camille continued to explain. Pointing out, "The cloths you wear, Vicki, sends a clear message. Not only that you take your job seriously. It also let others know that you demand to be taken seriously. The trick to this shit has always been looking the part. From your suit and shoes to your handbag let others know you mean business." Camille had Vicki model a few things and was sure Vicki would have a problem walking in the six-inch stilettos. Vicki, however, surprised her by taking to the sky-high heels as if she had been doing it for quite some time.

Camille had spent a small fortune assembling Vicki's new wardrobe with top-notch designers.

Over the next few days, Camille trained Vicki in hand to hand combat. She was taught the fundamentals of offensive boxing. Defensive jujitsu and karate. Then shown how to counter a strike. Camille also showed her where to locate seven major weak spots on the human body and how to strike them.

Once Vicki thought she was finally ready, Camille had something else in stored for her. It was her appearance. Mainly her hair. At first, Vicki had been opposed to the idea of giving up her corn-rows, but once Camille explained to her the role she was about to play called for it, Vicki relented.

After the makeover was completed, Vicki viewed her new look in the large wall mirror at the salon and was astound at how attractive she really was. Aside from her glamorized hair-style that managed to maintain her ethnocentricity. The contradistinction of her eye make-up didn't just accentuated her hazel eyes, it made them appear lighter in color.

Later that night, Camille schooled Vicki on the rules of becoming an assassin. "You remember when I told you about the rules you have to follow?"

"Yeah, but you never told me what the rules were?" Vicki laughed. "You make it sound like some kind of assassin association. Who the hell made rules for the murder game?"

"All professions have rules. With reference to assassins, never on public transportation, or a moving vehicles. Bars are definitely off limits unless of course the bar serves food. Then of course it's fair game."

"Of course." Vicki sarcastically inserted.

"Always remember patience is everything. The worst thing you can do is try to force a hit."

Vicki thought about it and remembered the night her husband tried to convince her to wait for another time to hit the mark, but she had been insistent. A decision that cost her everything. Had she listened to him? He and Ma'Matty would probably still be alive. Michael Henderson and his men, on the other hand, would still be dead.

As Camille continued, Vicki pushed her thoughts of self-pity back into the recesses of her mind and began paying close attention to everything Camille had to convey.

"One time..." Camille remembered staking out a target. "...I spent all afternoon at a bus-stop a few houses down from where the target lived. It was my forth assignment and a tough one. The target was a 'bag-man' for the mob who had been skimming from the top. My job was to hit him at his home. He lived in an apartment house in the suburb, making my job even harder. I scope the place out for a while before making my move. His apartment was on the top floor of a three-unit house and it seemed like every house on the block had a front-yard lined with thick, tall shrubs. The side-walks were clean, abandoned and lined with garbage cans, parked cars and trees on both sides of the street. It was a beautiful nice quiet neighborhood. The trees created a canopy up and down the one-way street as far as the eyes can see. I mean, absolutely no reason for someone to stop and loiter. Not to mention all the hiding places were on private property.

When I walked pass the house, my heart sunk. If things couldn't have gotten any worse, the target lived right next to a nursery-school. Which made the stakeout even harder because loitering anywhere near a nursery-school will attract cops, or worse, threatened mothers.

Around four P.M., parents start arriving to pick up their kids from the nursery. You shoulda' seen the way they eyed me."

"Did you leave?" Vicki curiously asked while wondering what she would have done in the same situation.

"Hell no. Shit, I had to get creative. I acted as if I was waiting on a bus. I ain't gonna' lie, though. It was exhausting and frustrating at the same time. The target never came out and a woman who had been walking her dog kept eyeing me suspiciously. I kept my head and remained calm. Still, I could  tell she knew something wasn't right? Fortunately I caught a break. The woman was just about to approach me when this short, sexy blond named, Emily came out of the same house the target was staying in and began flirting with me.

Vicki smiled when she asked, "What you do?"

"Used her hot lil' ass to get in. After that, you already know." Both women laughed.

"What about that old woman who had been watching you?"

"She eyed the both of us before going off about her business. Emily was a little older than me, but had the voice of a child. That was the only shit that turned me off about her. I recently saw her up here looking for work. When I heard Johnathen Crain Senior was interviewing for live-in care-givers. I immediately contacted her and had an interview set up. With her looks and that voice, I knew he wouldn't deny her the job. It's temporary, but it'll take care of her financial problems for a while."

"So she got the job?" Vicki wanted to be sure.

"Yeah. A few weeks later she told me a man by the name of Napoleon Webb came by to drop some important papers off. Because Emily was old man Crain's care giver, he thought it was important she knew that the old man has early on-set Alzheimer's. He also made her promise to never mention it to anyone. Not even Crain's own son, Junior. Before he left, Emily manage to sneak a peek at those important papers he brought over. She told me they were black and white sexually explicit photos of old white men with young children. Some were boys, but mostly girls. When I mentioned it to Cat. She immediately contacted someone she called, the antique dealer."

"Why an antique dealer?"

"I don't know if he was an actual antique dealer. It was just something she called him. I do know he was a professional thief, and not cheap either. He ultimately arranged to have the safe in Crain's house hit. Everything went according to plan until she went to retrieve the package."

"What happened?"

"The unthinkable. We learned the antique dealer was murdered the night before. Something about a robbery gone bad?"

"You got to be kidding. What happen to the photos?"

"According to Cat, the deal died with the Antique Dealer."

"You believed her?"

"Why shouldn't I? Cat and I go way back. She has no reason to lie. At least I don't think she does?"

"What were the two of you planning on doing with those photos?"

"Exposing old man Crain and his perverted partners. Now, I have to take another route."

Vicki frowned. "I don't understand?"

"You will."

The next morning, Vicki was still laying in bed sleeping when she was awaken by someone at the door. She was about to get out of bed to answer it when Camille rushed passed her. Dressed only in her bra and panties she yelled, "I got it!" It was the way Camille shot past the bed to answer the door that led Vicki to assume it was someone she had been expecting.

Vicki watched as Camille took a quick peep through the view-hole before opening the door. A tall, slim white woman walked in and sat on the sofa in the front room. When Camille sat next to her, Vicki sat up in bed to get a better look. She had a clear view of Camille, but could not see Camille's visitor.

As both women began to whisper. Vicki decided to give them some privacy. It was at that moment when Camille noticed Vicki getting out of bed. "Vicki! I want you to meet someone." Vicki was about to put something on when Camille rushed into the bed area and grabbed her by the arm, practically dragging her into the living area to meet her friend. "Vicki, this is Cat, the friend I was telling you about. Cat, this is Vicki."

The woman smiled politely and said, "Actually, it's Catherine. Cat is a short I no longer use these days. It's nice to finally meet you, Vicki."

"Hi. Camille has told me so much about you, I feel like I already know you." Vicki didn't know why, but for some reason she had pictured a younger looking woman.

Catherine smiled. "I hope it was all good," she said with a light laugh. "I was sorry to hear about your husband. I heard he was a good man. What was his name, Bull?"

Vicki stared at Catherine wondering how she could have known that? She then looked at Camille, who was now staring at Catherine with annoyance. "Bull was a pet name I gave him. Everyone called him, 'Face. Actually it was Baby-face because he looked so young. He hated being called that so out of respect everybody just called him

180

'Face instead. And think you, he was a good man." Vicki then looked at Camille. Who quickly stood and walked over to the closet to retrieve something.

When she returned to the sofa. She dropped a folder on top of the coffee table in front of Vicki and said, "Fail to plan, you plan to fail." Vicki picked up the folder and opened it. There was a photo and an extensive profile of a thirty-seven year old casually dressed street hustler named, Tyrone Sharp. There were also several other files and photos to match the individual being profiled.

Vicki looked at Camille somewhat confused. Then at Catherine, then back at the photo wondering why the sudden interest in FOLD members? She closed the folder and tossed it back on top of the table. She had no interest in reading any of the files. Especially Tyrone Sharp's. She considered him a friend and the last thing she wanted was to invade his privacy.

"Your boy Tyrone almost got himself killed last week," said Camille.

"Yes," Catherine interject. "He came to see me about my late husband's killers."

"That would be Henderson. Michael Henderson," said Camille. Vicki looked at her and silently thought, Another detail you neglected to mention.

"And I don't have to tell you what a nightmare that was," Catherine felt a need to share before continuing. "He tried to have me killed, you know. I only recently arrived back in town when I learned of his death."

"And who told you about that?" Vicki asked while staring at Camille. "Oh, let me guess, Camille filled you in?"

"Actually, no. I was informed by the very same man who was responsible," said Catherine.

Vicki was confused. Catherine noticed and smiled. Vicki immediately turned to Camille for answers.

"She's talking about Crain Junior," said Camille.

Vicki immediately changed the subject, "What about this?" she asked, grabbing the Intel file from the table, she held it in Camille's face. "You never said anything about this?"

"But I did tell you how important it was to know what and who you are dealing with. If you're worried about their safety, don't be. As far as I know, they're all safe." She paused, "Well... I can't speak for all of them. The young baller who likes to wear suits is another story."

"SunRise?"

"Yeah, him. He's manage to stay one step ahead of me. I can't seem to find him and neither can anyone else?"

Catherine immediately spoke up. "Tyrone has assured me, he...."

"Tyrone?" Vicki interrupted her.

"Yes. Tyrone Sharp."

Caught completely off guard, Vicki asked, "Why would Tyrone tell you anything about SunRise? You don't know him like that. Do you?"

Both women chuckled. "And then some," said Catherine. "As I was saying before we got off track. Tyrone came to see me not too long ago. He had some questions for me about Michael's killers. Apparently he was concerned about my safety. How sweet. Once I convinced him I didn't know anything, he left. Unfortunately he was spotted leaving by some very nasty people. Luckily he managed to lose them outside. But made the  mistake  of following them to Junior's apartment in Manhattan. Of course they caught him."

"Yeah," Camille jumped in. "When he decided to follow those men, I followed him. Lucky for him I saw when they rolled up  on him. I was watching from the roof of a building across the street and gave Junior a call to warn him that, if something should happen to Mr. Sharp, he would be the first to get it in the head. I told him to hand the phone to, Mr. Sharp. Once Sharp was on the line, I advised him to leave."

Vicki held up the folder and asked, "Where did you get this?"

"Out of Sharp's car the night I saved his life. He took it from Crain, who got it from Sharp's lawyer."

"I don't understand?" Vicki was even more confused now.

"The reason your friends are being tracked by Junior is because Tyrone's lawyer betrayed him."

"His lawyer?"

"Former lawyer. By the time I could warn him. He, his wife and her nurse were all dead and his computer, gone. Junior had him murdered because he knew too much."

"What was on the computer?" Vicki quickly asked.

"Camille briefly glanced at Catherine and said, "It's a long story that had something to do with a disk Tyrone and his friends stole from Junior. They gave it to their lawyer who was suppose to give it to the Feds in exchange for the immunity of one of their friends." Camille then looked at Catherine. "Cat will see to it Tyrone stays out of trouble. As for your other friend? What did you call him?"

"SunRise. What about him?" asked Vicki."

"Yeah, Him. I don't think Junior have a file on him. Hopefully he's not a target."

"Yes" Catherine quickly jumped in. "We were hoping maybe he made a copy of the disk?"

Vicki looked at Catherine and asked, "What disk? Where's Tyrone Sharp right now?"

Catherine looked at her watch and said, "Getting ready to give me a pedicure in about five minutes."

Vicki then turned to Camille and asked, "He should know where to find SunRise?"

"According to Cat, he doesn't."

Vicki turned back to Catherine for answers.

"Don't look at me," said Catherine.

Vicki placed the folder back on the table and stood. "Then I don't know what to tell you. Except wherever he is? You can believe he's on top of his game." She then walked off into the bathroom.

Camille looked at Catherine and asked, "What time did you say Junior was gonna' be at his father's house tomorrow?"

"Around six in the evening. Why?"

"It's time to end this. In the mean time, I suggest you and Tyrone lay low."

Just as Vicki returned wearing a robe, Catherine gave Camille a naughty smiled and replied, "I plan to. Right between his legs."

"Just be careful. I know you really like him and all, but he's a target. If Junior's men see him, he could place you in danger?"

"Oh no, darling. He has a safe house we'll be staying at."

"Then I suggest the two of you stay there until you hear from me, or Vicki. No going out. You hear?" Camille warned.

"We'll be fine, Sweetheart. I plan on keeping him quite busy between my legs." she giggled. "He's crazy about me, you know."

Camille and Vicki looked at one another. "I'm going to give you a number," Camille said while jotting it down on a piece of scrap paper. "The first chance you get once you're at the safe-house, call it. We need to know where to find you," said Camille.

Catherine smiled while looking over the number. She then looked up at Vicki and said, "It was nice meeting you, Vicki," before leaving.

"Same here," Vicki replied under her breath. She looked at Camille and said, "She must have sucked his dick?" while trying to picture Tyrone Sharp and Catherine Henderson together in bed. For some reason, she couldn't. She didn't know Tyrone Sharp all that well, but was under the impression he was a 'black militant' like his comrades. According to Catherine Henderson, he was an undercover freak with either a sweet tooth for white meat, or a bad case of 'Jungle-fever'. Either way, Vicki silently thought, he was faking jacks.

# CHAPTER 12

Later that evening, Camille sent Vicki out recruiting soldiers. In order to accomplish their goal, both women knew they were going to need a thorough team. It was the second time Vicki had actually been out on her own since the nervous break-down. After meeting Camille, she felt great about herself and much more confident.

Every so often she would think about the first time she met her husband and mother-in-law. It was the one memory of them she cherished most. She had Camille to thank for helping her out of her depression. But for some reason not fully understood, she didn't completely trust Camille. She couldn't quite put her finger on it, but she couldn't help feeling there was something Camille wasn't telling her.

As Vicki headed up town in Camille's rental. She thought of someone she had the pleasure of meeting at her husband's burial. She didn't know him personally, but something told her he'd be perfect for the job. There was something cold and heartless about him she really liked. His name was Bilaal, but the streets knew him as, 'Ghost'.

On her way towards Governor Street, his words rung in her head over and over again, "If you need me in any way, shape, or form, I'll be staying in town on Governor Street." She knew trying to actually find him would be a long shot, but she had to try.

Vicki drove up and down Governor Street a few times until finally turning off on Gram Avenue. Almost immediately she spotted someone to whom she knew could lead her to the man she was looking for. Her name was, Maria Africa. Maria was standing outside of a local pool-hall as if she was waiting for someone.

After parking, Vicki got out of the car and hurried across the street towards the pool-hall.

"MARIA!" she called out to the short, petite woman with bushy, red, dreadlocks. At first, the woman didn't recognize Vicki at all. But when she smiled, Vicki saw the recollection in her eyes.

"Hey, girl! You look so different, I almost didn't recognize you." she looked at Vicki from head to toe in complete awe. "Why such a radical change?"

"You like it?"

"It's nice. Different, but nice. I haven't seen you since the funeral. How you holding up, girl?" Maria was an attractive dark skinned, petite woman with prominent African features. About five feet tall with no inches and barely weighing a hundred pounds. She was in her fifties, yet managed to retain a youthful appearance of forty, or so. Vicki had met her through some people she knew at her husband's funeral. Adamantly revered by those whose opinions mattered, Vicki took an instant liking to her.

"I've been going through it, but I'm good now. Just have to get back on my J-O-B, you know?"

"I know that's right. These catz' out here think you lost your nerve. You know how they are. They loved your husband and want to make it right. The thing is, no one knows what happen, or who's responsible? No one but you, feel me?" She stared at Vicki with intense, piercing eyes. There was something dark and calculating about her that made Vicki like her even more.

"The only thing I lost, was my husband. If anyone's gonna' make it right, that be me."

Maria smiled. "I know that's right," she said. She had heard so much about Vicki's reputation, but the women she met at the funeral was a far cry from the woman who stood in front of her now. "So what brings you out here so late on a Saturday evening? You didn't strike me as the partying type?"

Vicki came straight to the point. "I'm looking for your friend, Ghost? At least I am assuming the two of you are friends? I saw you talking with him at my husband's funeral. Please tell me you know who I'm talking about?"

"I know him. He and my husband are partner. I'm waiting for my husband now," she looked down the street past Vicki in search of her husband. "He shoulda' been here by now," she thought aloud before looking at Vicki again and smiling. "I just can't get over how good you look, girl. I mean, you just took the word, gorgeous to a whole new level."

Vicki blushed. "You really think it's me?"

"With that body, girl, and those eyes of yours. Any look you chose would work." When Maria heard someone call her name, she looked past Vicki and smile. "Here he comes now," she said, referring to her husband. When Vicki turned around and saw the man Maria referred to as her husband approaching, her heart skipped a beat. "Vicki, this is my husband, Bomani. Baby, this is Vicki. Her husband was, 'Face." Maria cordially introduced the two.

Bomani  extended his hand. "Oh, yeah," he said with recollection. "How you doing, sista'? I don't know if you remember me. I never really got a chance to meet you at the funeral. Sorry for your lost. I didn't know your husband personally. He was just a pup when I left."

"I think I recall seeing you there." Vicki studied his face. She could not believe Baxter Keys and this man were not the same person. She remembered Londell mentioning him as Big Keys, Baxter older brother and a ferocious beast when he needed to be. I wonder how he and Maria met? she thought to herself. Physically, they were total opposites and seemed like an unlikely couple. He was tall, about 6'4", 255 pounds of solid muscle and very light in skin-tone. Vicki guessed him to be in his late thirties, but could have been older. Like Maria, he also wore dreadlocks. His, however were long, thick, rope-like that had to be over ten years old. From what Londell had told her about him. She prayed he never learned the truth about his kid brother. He seemed like a nice person. She would hate to go to war with him over something that couldn't be avoided.

"You a'ight, sista'?" he asked when he noticed Vicki staring.

Maria also noticed Vicki's preoccupation with a distant thought. "Yeah, Vicki. You look like you just saw a ghost, or some shit."

"Naw, um' good," Vicki was quick to assure the couple. "It's just... never mind."

"You sure you a'ight?" Maria felt the need to asked once more just to be sure.

"Positive," Vicki said with assurance before turning to Bomani, "You know where I can find your boy, Ghost?"

"If I tell him you wanna' see him? He'll find you.

"I doubt that. I don't get out much these days. I do need to see him. It's important."

"I'll let him know."

"I'm staying at the...."

"Alexander on Church Street. I got you, sista'" Bomani finished her sentence for her.

Vicki stood there speechless as he affectionately placed his arm around Maria's neck before the two of them walked off. Maria turned and shouted back at Vicki, "See you, Vicki!"

"How the fuck did he know where I was staying?" Vicki wondered while watching as the tall man stroll up the street with his arm affectionately wrapped around Maria's neck.

At seventy-two years of age, Johnathen Crain Senior mostly stayed to himself these days. When his health became an issue. His wife insisted he retire from the draining demanding of business. He later had the summer home he bright for her, converted into a year-round. Making it their full-time residence.

After his wife passed, he became somewhat of a recluse. Choosing to live out the rest of his days in solitude at the enlarged summer cape style home in Litchfield, northwestern Connecticut. Leaving the twenty million dollar Hillside Manor, also located in Connecticut, to his son, Junior.

He loved the small, modest home he originally bought for his late wife. Mostly because it reminded him so much of her. She loved it for its location. In walking distance of Litchfield, one of Connecticut's most colorful historic villages. The house sat on a reclusive lot, affording a certain amount of privacy. There was even a brook traversing the yard. On occasions, the old man would invite his son, Junior over for dinner, or drinks. Mostly they would talk business. Especially with the trouble Junior had been having lately. The lost of a large shipments in Queens. Eliminating five productive producers. One of which he murdered on a mere suspicion that he may have leaked vital information. Not to omit the lost of several more men at the apartment in lower Manhattan, and two old friends, Spurlock and Bobby White. Junior was beginning to bring unwanted attention to the Crain name and he didn't like it one bit.

A few hours after speaking with Maria and her husband, the desk-clerk called to inform Vicki there were some people asking for her. "Send them right up," she instructed. Upon her visitor's arrival, she was surprise to see Ghost, Bomani and Maria.

"You wanted to see me?" asked Ghost.

"I don't know if this is such a good idea," Vicki noted while gesturing the trio to come in. Once everyone was seated, she continued. "As you may have heard, I'm trying to put together a team. After my husband died, I was in a bad place. Literally lost the will to go on. Shortly thereafter, I lost my mother-in-law. But the night she passed she came to me in a dream. She talked about life and purpose and told me in order to find my purpose in life, I had to leave. Go out into the world and whatever life has in store for me? It will reveal itself. I left and it has. Before any of you decide to put your life on the line for me and my husband's killers. Understand this, you may not return from this mission. The 'marks' we are about to go up against aren't from the streets like us. They're from the jungles of Saigon. Trained by the United States Government in Guerilla warfare. They're mercenaries hired as a security team for a rich piece-of-shit name, Johnathen Crain Jr. Now... before I continue. I completely understand if any of you feel the need to leave?"

Vicki paused to await their decision. When no one elected to leave, she walked to the closet and retrieve a file on the subjects in question. First, she handed Ghost a file on Johnathen Crain Senior. After Ghost had a chance to scan the file, he passed it to his team. Vicki then hand him a file on Johnathen Crain Junior. The next file was on Ross, who Vicki estimate would have at least, ten to twelve men in teams of two to three.

"There will be four to six men securing the grounds. Two to three in the front and back. Same thing on the second floor level. We have to assume a few will be inside with Ross and the Crains."

"Why so much security for just a casual visit?" Bomani asked.

"There was an assault at Junior's apartment in lower Manhattan. They're gonna' be on the defensive. They lost a lot of men that night," Vicki said before moving on. She walked into the bedroom and returned with three vests, and three small, portable headset devises for communication purposes. "For your safety, it's important we remain in constant communication. Our objectives are the Crains. We'll have a sniper using a fifty cal' with armor piercing rounds. The sniper will try to take out most, if not all of their ground and second floor security. Clearing the way for us to advance inside the residence."

"So it's not just us? We have others on our team?" asked Maria.

"Just one other," Vicki told them while producing a chart she had drawn up. When she spread the chart out on top of the coffee table, everyone gathered around. The chart gave them a visual picture of the house and a geographical layout of the surrounding grounds of the Cape-style property in Connecticut where the assault was to take place. "We'll be using assault rifles with special fitted silencers. However, each of you are required to have a hand gun of your

194

choosing as back-up." She looked at Ghost and asked, "What type of weapon do you favor, Ghost?"

"A fifty caliber Desert Eagle, seven rounds, semi auto. Why? Is there a problem?"

"Not unless you're worried about it jamming on you." She turned her attention to Bomani and asked, "What about you, Bomani?"

Bomani smiled while producing a three-fifty-seven Magnum. "Never leave home without it."

"It's not too heavy for you? The recoil, I mean. It's a powerful gun?"

"I'm a powerful man," he replied while glancing at his wife Maria with a closed-mouth-smile.

"I know that's right," Maria said approvingly.

"Your turn, Maria," said Vicki.

Maria pulled out two snub nose, Walter PPK-nine millimeter with ten shots each and said, "I know you already heard how I get down."

Okay. I told you we already have someone watching the place. Hopefully they can tell us what we'll be dealing with before we arrive. Just remember, when you shoot, go lethal. All head shots if possible. If not? Assume they're wearing armor  and take out the limbs. Wear black. No coats, so dress warm. You never no how long we'll be out in the field."

"You said something about assault rifles?" asked Bomani.

"AK's. Less risk of having any problems. Any other questions before we wrap this up? Good. We meet outside this hotel tomorrow around five on the P.M. side. So remember, all black. Don't wear anything that might constrict you from movement and dress warm."

Catherine had been sitting in the lobby when Maria, Ghost and Bomani stepped off the elevator. As soon as she saw Bomani, she immediately stood and targeted him. "Excuse me?" When the trio of old school killers stopped, Catherine quickly spoke up, "Are you Big Keys?"

"Who's asking?" Maria immediately spoke up.

"I'm Catherine. I was referred to you by Asmar? You might know him as, Mr. Bang?" When no one answered, she asked another question. "He did speak to you about me, didn't he?" She fearfully looked from one to the other hoping for confirmation.

"Yeah. He spoke to us about you," Bomani said before looking at Maria and Ghost. "Y'all go ahead. I'll catch up with you later."

After Maria and Ghost left the hotel. Catherine led Bomani into the hotel lounge so they could talk in privacy.

# CHAPTER 13

The following morning, Catherine checked out of her suite and waited out front for Tyrone to take her to the safe house. It did not take long before she spotted the white BMW pulling up in front of the hotel.

When Tyrone got out to open the car-door for her, she smiled. Pleased with herself, she couldn't remember the last time she had been treated so nicely. Which was why she deliberately took her time getting in. Once she was in, he gathered her bags and placed them in the trunk.

While getting into the car, he noticed Michael Henderson's prized Ford Mustang pulling onto Church Street. He looked at Catherine while starting the car and asked, "Isn't that your husband's ride?"

She turned in her seat and saw the candy-apple red Mach III parking. "Give me a minute, sweetheart," she said while exiting the car. Asmar was on his way inside the hotel when she called out to him. Appropriately dressed in an all red crunch-leather sweat-suit. Red snake-skin tennis shoes. A red three quarter inch 'bubble goose' and a red base' cap tilted to the back. He stomped towards her as if the world was his.

"Damn, Ms. Catherine," he complained. "You was about to leave me hanging like that?"

"You know I'm on a time schedule, Mr. Bang. What took you so long? I called you over an hour ago. You know what... never mind," she said with apparent frustration while fidgeting around in her hand-bag until she found what she had been looking for. "As we agreed," she hand him what appeared to be the title and registration to the car he had been driving. When she saw Tyrone getting out of the car. She immediately pulled Asmar off to the side and began secretly whispering.

Tyrone watched with suspicious eyes. When he saw her handing Asmar an envelope, his jaw dropped. He wanted to say something, but knew he was probably over-reacting. Tyrone continue to watch as Asmar nodded in acknowledgment while assuring Catherine that he would take care of it. Asmar then looked at Tyrone and gave him a courtesy nod before leaving. On the brink of a jealous rage, Tyrone angrily got back into the car with a tight jaw and clinched paws.

As soon as Catherine was back inside the car, he angrily looked at her and asked, "You wanna' tell me what that was all about?"

"The end of a business relationship," she replied before elaborating in detail. "Mr. Bang and I go way back. He's been a very good friend who has had my back since I've known him."

"And how long have you known him? He must be big on you?" Tyrone felt the need to point out while pulling off.

"Actually," she went on to say, "he's been a perfect gentleman. Not once have he ever tried to get in my panties." She giggled at the thought of what she had just said.

"I don't believe that."

Flattered by his obvious jealousy, she smiled and said, "I never said he didn't want anything. I said he didn't want me."

"So what did he want, money?"

"No. Just Michael's prize possession. His car. That was the title you saw me giving him."

He smiled. It was at that moment when he realized just how badly he had fallen for this woman. A woman he practically knew nothing about. The night he had been abducted by Junior men, he learned something very significant about himself. He was not cut-out for the type of work SunRise required of him and wanted out. Especially after meeting her. He looked at her as if he was seeing her for the very first time.

She looked at him and smile. "What?" she asked, reaching over to rub his thigh.

"Nothing. I was just thinking about the night I first saw you in the hotel lobby."

"Yeah. What about it?"

"You were on your way to the desk. Remember? I called out to you?"

"I remember, sweetheart."

"Right then and there,' he continued. "I thought you were the finest woman I ever saw."

She giggled and caressed his crotch. "You're so sweet," she purred. When she felt him getting excited, she added, "and so hard, too."

"I have to be honest with you, baby."

"By all means, please do."

"Just thinking about you excites me."

She giggled some more while caressing his hardness.

"I don't know what it is about you, but you have that kind of effect on me."

Still stroking him, she blushed but did not say anything. She wanted to tell him, she had that kind of effect on all men. After all, it was part of her charm. But knew that would have been like telling him he was just one of many who had been riveted by her presence. Although there had been times she tried to convince herself she really liked him. But the truth was, he, like all the other men who've had the misfortune of coming into her life. Were nothing more than a sexual object.

She smiled as she began thinking about the first time she had saw him in the lobby. She thought he was a god and almost dropped to her knees right then and there. She remembered sitting there listening to him as he spoke. Half of what he had been saying went in one ear and out the other. She had been too preoccupied trying to envision what wonders he held for her between his legs. At one point, she thought about peeking but couldn't risk getting caught. A few times, she did manage to steal a peek. She wasn't sure if he had noticed and didn't care. She had to have that mental image of him. Something to get her through the night. At least until she could come up with an appropriate enough excuse to get him to bless her with his presence once more.

She remembered the difficult time she had squeezing Camille for his number. Once she had it, she wasn't sure whether or not to call. She didn't want to appear presumptuous. Most men didn't like women who were too forward and scaring him off was the last thing she wanted. "So where's your hide-out?" she finally asked. The mere thought of being alone with him again made her warm and moist between her legs.

"Somewhere no one will find us unless we want to be found. Not even my friends know about this spot." Truth be told, he didn't want to be found. He just wanted to be alone with her. Which was why he rented the love-nest located just outside of Paterson in the small quiet town called, Little Falls. "There's something you should know about me," he changed the subject. "but before I bare my soul I need to know something from you?"

She apprehensively looked at him. Her first thoughts were, he had managed to find out about her past.

"I need to know where you see us going as a couple? Better yet, where would you like to see it go?"

Relieved, she smiled and slid close to him. "It's been a long time since I had a man I really wanted to be with, Tyrone. I'm not a young woman anymore. Nor am I too old to have children," she glanced at him before continuing. "Before I met you, I thought I would always be the other woman. To be honest with you. I thought you'd just turn out to be a fling. That is, of course, until we slept together. You didn't just fuck me, sweetheart. You made love to me. I never felt so special in my life. If that's how you treat all your women, you should have been a pimp."

He glanced at her oddly. "A pimp! Damn! I didn't expect to hear you say that," he couldn't help but to wonder where that came from? "Shit. You the type of woman who could probably have any man you want? Instead, you chose me. Not that I'm putting myself down, or anything. I just never dreamt you would even be remotely interested in a raw cat like me?"

She snuggled up to him. "That's how I like my man, sweetheart. That's how I like my man to give it to me. Raw." She didn't mean to be so forward. At least not so soon. "I hope that doesn't scare you?" she looked at him. "Does it? Scare you, I mean?"

"Hell to the no! That kinda' shit turn me the fuck on. The thing is... if my friends saw me with a white woman? They wouldn't understand. I told you about the organization I work for, didn't I?"

"Worked for," she corrected him.

"Yeah... worked for. I've been a hustler all my life until meeting, SunRise. Now that I'm severing all ties with FOLD, I don't know what we gonna' do for money?" He glanced at her and smiled.

She returned his smile and laid her head on his shoulder. "Darling?" she spoke with a soft moan.

"Yeah, baby, what's up?" he asked without taking his eyes from the road.

"I have to tell you something. Please don't be upset with me, but you remember the copy of that disk Junior kept asking you about?"

He glanced at her strangely while wondering how she could know that. "What about it?"

"Junior's father's off-shore account number were on that disk. There's enough money in the accounts to buy a private Island and build a resort on it. I overheard Junior telling one of his men that your lawyer was suppose to give the disk to the Fed?"

"Yeah. Stupid ass-hole gave the thing to your boy and probably got himself killed."

"I'm almost certain Junior destroyed it. But if there's a copy? We can still give it to the Fed after draining the accounts. Think about it, darling. Just the two of us living a life of luxury while Junior and his family rots in some federal prison cell."

"How much money we talking about? Better yet, how the hell do you know all this?" he asked out of pure curiosity. The status of his interest on the topic was merely an indulgence out of boredom and nothing more. As far as he was concern, that disk had been the bane of his existence. if he never saw it again, was more than fine with him.

"I know because it took me almost twenty years to get the information to created the disk. There is a little over two-hundred million in that account."

He choked. "WHAT!"

"Just think, sweetheart. Being waited on hand and foot. It's a dream, darling. A dream we can live together."

Not sure if he believed her, he glanced at her and said, "Damn that's a lot of money. You serious, or just blowing smoke up my ass? Better yet, how the hell did you get the information on that disk?"

"It's a long boring story, but if we can get our hands on that copy. Our grandchildren well be set for life." She laid her head on his shoulder and smiled while lightly rubbing between his legs. She could tell he liked the sound of her last statement.

"We just have to get our hands on that copy." Tyrone muttered to himself. He specifically remembered BeeBop retrieving the copy of the disk for SunRise at the apartment the day SunRise returned from his trip to South Jersey.

She lift her head to look at him. "Are you saying there is a copy?" she asked with hopefulness in her voice.

"Yeah, but getting our hands on it gonna' be a bitch. I can't believe I had that much money in my hand and gave it to that dumb ass lawyer. DAMN! I could kick myself in the ass." He looked at her again and asked, "You ain't fucking with me, are you? I mean, you serious about this shit, or what?"

"Yes I'm serious. So you're sure there's a copy?"

"Positive. SunRise has it and I don't think he's just gonna' give it up."

She laid her head back on his shoulder and smiled. "I think we'll be just fine, sweetheart."

He glanced down at her. "I don't know why you say that? You don't know 'Rise."

Catherine secretly thought, "He's a man, isn't he?" With her head still resting on his shoulder, she smelt his cologne. He smelt good to her. She wanted to smell his crotch, but knew that was the whore coming out of her. She closed her eyes and visualize him lightly pulling her hair while hitting it from the back. She loved it that way and was pleased with herself for training him to satisfy her perverted sexual needs. She visualized his hard, naked body and felt a warm tingle between her legs. "We almost there, sweetheart?" she asked. There was a fire burning deep within her that desperately needed to be satisfied.

"Yeah, baby. We're almost there."

# NEMESIS III

# CHAPTER 14

Wrestling with the easiest way to break the news to her new crew. Vicki stood outside of the Alexander Hotel waiting on her trio of old-school killers. The moment she had gotten word the mission had been scratched, she was relieved. The three were hardly what she considered a strike-team. Still, she just didn't have the heart to turn them away. Which made her realize something very significant about herself. She was getting soft. Had Camille not called to abandon the mission. Vicki would have not only sacrifice her life and the lives of her friends, but also the success of the mission. Even now as she stood waiting on her crew she felt awkward about braking the bad news to them. Camille never gave an explanation for the sudden change in plans. Which made Vicki's task of breaking the bad news to her crew all the more difficult.

A half hour would pass before Vicki suddenly realized the trio was a 'no-show'. Any other time she might have been upset. This, however, was one of those rear occasions she felt relieved. Disappointed, but relieved. She had never worked with any of the three, but was sure they would have been out of their league going up against Ross and his men.

She was about to go back into the hotel when she noticed Michael Henderson's red Ford Mustang turn onto Church Street. Curious as to who the driver might be, she continued to watch until the driver parked. As soon as she saw Asmar West exiting the car, she quickly stepped into the hotel. She didn't know Asmar personally. He was a friend of Joey Lemon, who was a friend of her late husband. What little she did seem to know about him, left a bitter taste in her mouth. Mostly because he gave her the impression he was the type of person who stayed in everyone else's business. She knew she could have been wrong about him, but that was the impression he gave her.

On her way to the elevator, she stopped when she heard someone call her name. When she turned around and saw Asmar quickly approaching, she suddenly regretted having stopped.

"DAMN!" he observed while looking her over very carefully. "I wasn't sure if it was you." he said, still staring. "You look good as hell, Ma'. DANM!"

"What's on your mind?" she coldly asked, wondering what could he possibly want with her?

"There's a six forty-five flight leaving this evening from JFK to New Orleans International. I gotta' first class ticket for you. Ms. Catherine told me to tell you your friend will be waiting for you at Kennedy in one hour." He hand her one first-class ticket and told her not to worry about checking out of her suite. "I was told to tell you your friend took care of it." He looked at his watch and said, "I can have you there in thirty-five minute?"

"I need at least twenty to pack?"

"A'ight, but that's cutting it kinda' close. I'll be up in ten minutes to help you with your bags. I have to move my car. I'm double parked." he said before dashing off.

"Your car?" Vicki mumbled under her breath.

Asmar drove around the corner onto Market Street and park. Instead of getting out of the car. He reached up under the leather seat and retrieved a small, plastic bag of Purple Haze. Then pulled a Fonta leaf from the pocket of his coat to roll it.

While he sat there twisting up. He noticed a familiar face coming up the street in his direction. The face belonged to a man the streets knew as, E-Man. An old-school, ex-addict and stick-up kid from the 1970's. E-Man was now a bouncer at a strip-joint down town called the 'Cheaters Club'. Some say he was trying to walk the straight and narrow by staying clear of trouble.

Asmar briefly took his eyes off of E-Man long enough to lined the leaf with the Haze. After twisting it up. He brought the freshly rolled spliff to his mouth and thoroughly lick it. He then placed it between his lips and lit it. He took a few pulls before popping open the glove compartment to grab the pearl grip of his chrome plated forty-five.

Just before E-Man reached the car. Asmar cocked a round in the chamber and laid the gun on his lap so the familiar face would be sure to see it. He then took two more long, hard pulls from the spliff before sitting it in the ash-tray. He cracked the window to air the car out of all the trapped smoke that had accumulated while formulating the game he was about to push up under his ol'head prey.

Asmar was the type of guy who could insinuate his way into your life so casually. Before you knew it, you'd be calling him, cuz'. A predator of sort, he instinctively used people for personal gain and never gave the consequences of his actions a second thought. As far as he was concerned, it was all about him.

Once he began to feel the effects of the designer weed. He retrieved the spliff from the ash-tray and took another hit before catching a glimpse of his reflection in the rear-view. Captivated by his own reflection, he completely forgotten all about E-Man. When, without an invitation. E-Man got into the car from the passenger side.

E-Man was an impatient cat whose chronicles as a proficient trick-boxer during his youth had been legendary. Back in the day when cat wore afros, black leather jackets and called Stacey Adams, Old-Man-Comfort, E-Man ran with P-Town's notorious hoods. In and out of jail, he finally got tired of chasing his own tail and turned his life around, so to speak. As a full time bouncer. He had a long list of things he could have been doing oppose to wasting his time with what he considered, a pot-head prankster who fancied himself as a gangster.

As Asmar exhaled the smoke from his lungs, he coughed a little before speaking. Yo, whaz' good, yo?"

"You tell me? Five catz' done told me you been asking 'bout my business?"

"Yeah whatever, yo. Check this out, you remember last year when they found your brother dead? They ever find out what happened to him?" Asmar adjusted the gun on his lap just in case E-Man hadn't noticed it yet.

"Why?" E-Man asked with two narrowing eyes.

"I wanna' know if that reward you offered last year was still on the table? Jokers like me gotta' eat, too. You feel me?"

He stared at Asmar for a moment with suspicious eyes. "You know it is. Otherwise you wouldn't be asking around," he replied before asking. "You know something 'popo don't?"

"You know I do. Otherwise you wouldn't be sitting in my ride wasting your valuable time." Asmar studied his expression before continuing. "The offer was ten grand, righ'?"

E-Man's face twisted into an angry frown. "Don't play games with me, young'en. The offer was and still is, five, cash!"

Asmar looked at his watch and realized he was running late. "I hope you can peel mine off right now, 'cause I don't have time to negotiate a payment plan. I need mine up front before...."

"Do I look like um' worried about a joker like you crossing me?" he cut Asmar off before pulling out his wallet to produce a thick stack of bills. As far as Asmar could tell, they were all hundreds. Once E-Man strategically counted out five thousand. He tossed the bills onto Asmar's lap over the gun. Asmar smiled and went to reach for the bills, but froze when he felt the cold nozzle of his own .45 pressed firmly against his cheek.

"What the..." The thought of his life being in danger wasn't his main concern. He was more eager to know how E-Man managed to get his gun so easily. "How the fuck you do that, yo'?"

"Before you touch my money, young'en. You betta' gim'me the impression you earned it?"

"I got you, yo! Slow the fuck down for you make a mistake and shoot yourself. Feel me?"

At exactly six P.M., Johnathen Crain Jr. arrived at his Father's Connecticut home in Litchfield with the head of his security, Roger Ross and several of Ross' men. Personally, Junior thought the six men Ross had accompanying them was a bit excessive, but his father had been insistent.

"One could never be too careful," he remembered his father stressing. He knew his father was concerned about the problems he had been having lately. He, on the other hand was more concerned in knowing how his father had manage to find out about his personal business so quickly. And though he had his suspicions? It was too early to prove his theory just yet.

While Junior and his father sat in the front room sipping on a Razz Mint Martini. Roger Ross stood close by, alert and on point. He couldn't quite put his finger on it, but something just wasn't quite right. He had a nose for smelling trouble. Which was why he wanted to bring more security along. But Junior thought the six men he had already deployed around the property was more than sufficient.

"I have a surprise for you, son," said the old man.

"A surprise?"

"The shipment from the house in Regal Park the police confiscated somehow disappeared from property."

"What do you mean, disappeared?"

"Perhaps disappeared was a poor choice of words. Let's just say the Regal Park shipment has been replaced with something similar in appearance. Hardly what anyone would call a narcotic. In other words, you have your shipment back. The commissioner is an old friend of your godfather."

"Napo'?"

"They go as far back when the commissioner was just a cop walking the beat. Napo' and I were instrumental in helping him with his career. You might say he owes us more than just a favor."

"Thank you, father."

"It was a good thing we heard about your troubles when we did. Otherwise it might have been too late to called in the favor."

"But father! I...." Junior protested.

The old man held up his hand, stopping his son from denying responsibility. "Your business is your business, son. Napo' and I do not approve of you implicating the family name with drugs, but what's done is done. The bottom line, you were responsible for the shipment. Somehow the locals found out about it. For god's sake son," the old man paused to cough. "at least be a man and take responsibility for your inability to handle what was supposed to be a simple transaction." Clearly the old man was beginning to get up-set, but manage to regain his composure.

Junior held his head down in shame. He knew his father was right, but like his father so eloquently put it. What was do, was done. "So when and where can I recover the shipment, father?" Junior asked.

"The shipment is here, son. But I want it out when you leave tonight, understood?"

Junior smiled with a sense of relief. "I understand, father." Everything was coming back together for him. The best part was; his father knew nothing about the disk he managed to retrieve from Melvin Vincent. And because he had destroyed it along with the people who created it. His father will never learn of its existence.

"As I was saying," the old man was about to continue when a short, young, attractive woman with curly blond hair walked into the room.

"Dinner is served, Sir," she announced, then left. Both Junior and Ross looked at the woman strangely. Physically it was clear she was not a minor. Her voice, however, could easily give you the impression she was. As Junior continued to stare at the woman, he couldn't help but to wondered where his father had found her?

"We'll continue this conversation after dinner," said the old man. Junior was about to assist his father out of the chair when the old man reached for Ross. Who immediately rushed over to help the old man up. While the old man leaned on Ross for support. Junior stood angrily watching. The simple act of kindness he had just witness between Ross and his father was proof positive he was being out maneuvered. Apparently, he wasn't the only employer Ross was collecting a check from. Ross had been playing both sides of the street and Junior did not appreciate being thought of as a fool. Still, he couldn't worry about that now. He would deal with Ross once they were out of the company of his father.

Junior was just about to join Ross and his father in the dinning-room. When he heard something that sounded like a thump right outside. He walked over to the window and eased back the curtain to peered out. It was dark, but he could have sworn he saw some movement out in the distance. He walked over to the front door, opened it and stepped outside. He had expected to see  some of his security team Ross had deployed around the property. Oddly enough, no one was anywhere to be seen. He was about to check  around back until he felt a stinging pain to his ear-lobe. He immediately grabbed his ear, but when he looked at his hand and saw the blood. He suddenly realized he was being shot at.

As terror began to grip him, he maneuvered his way back to the front door. Stopping momentarily to duck as silent bullets chipped chunks of wood from the side of the house.

He ran back into the house and quickly closed the door behind him. On his hands and knees he eased over to the window, peeled back the curtain and peeked out. First he saw the street lights on the main road go out. Out into the distant darkness he saw the muzzle flashes as bullets quietly ate away at the front of the house. Ross had strategically deploy six men around the property. Miraculously, they all somehow just disappeared?

He backed away from the window and could hear an onslaught of bullets chipping away at the front of the house. By the time he reached the dinning-room, he was beside himself. "WE'RE BEING ATTACKED!" he all but screamed while holding a blood-soaked handkerchief to his right ear.

"WHAT?" Ross immediately stood and pulled out his weapon.

"They're outside shooting at the house!"

Ross rushed into the front room and proceeded to peeked out the window. It was pitch dark outside. "Call the police!" he yelled to Junior while trying to contact his men on the ear communication headset. When no one answered, he had to assume they were all dead.

"The line's dead!" Junior cried from across the room.

Ross was about to rushed back into the dinning-room when he saw several shadows creeping up to the house. "Kill all the lights!" he shouted. Once all the lights in the house were out, he peeked out the window again. The shadows were in clear view now. He only counted three armed assassins, but was sure there were many more. Carefully he took aim and shot five rounds, "POP! POP! POP! POP! POP!" He thought he might have hit one, but couldn't really be sure. Nor was he sure how many men he was up against. One thing he was sure of? If they were going to survive the assault on the house, he needed help and heavier fire power. He peeked out the window again, but did not see anything, or anyone. There were no bodies lying on the ground. Which led him to believe he missed. "Mr. Crain!" he shouted. Junior appeared in the front-room crawling on his belly. "If you're going to make it through this," he pointed out. "We need help. NOW!"

"What do you want me to do?" Junior frantically asked.

"Where's your father?"

"Still in the dinning-room. I told him to stay under the table."

"And the girl? Find the girl." When Junior hesitated, Ross shouted, "MOVE IT!"

While Junior crawled off into the kitchen where the young female had been last seen. Ross eased the curtains back and glanced out the window again. He squinted his eyes and scanned the perimeter for any movement until he saw something. He couldn't quite make out exactly what it was. Just dark shadows moving about in formation.

"I see you. You motherfuckers. I see your asses now," he muttered under his breath while taking aim. He was about to shoot when all of a sudden the shadows seem to multiply. "What the hell?" he uttered while backing away from the window. Before leaving the area, he glanced back at the window and saw shadows approaching all around the house. "Everybody!" he shouted on his way back into the dining area. "We have to move." He looked under the table and grabbed the old man by the arm and pulled him out. "Mr. Crain? Where is your son?" As the old man got to his feet, he looked around fearfully. "Come on," Ross told him. "We have to get you up stairs."

As Ross and the old man made their way up the steps. Junior was on his way down. "The girl isn't in the house. She's gone!"

"GONE! What the hell do you mean, gone?" asked Ross.

"She's not in the house. I looked everywhere. She must have left? She's probably dead by now. I looked out the window from my father's room. I didn't see anyone? Where the hell are all your men? WE HAVE TO GET OUT OF HERE!" yelled Junior.

Ross yelled back, "AND GO WHERE! Our vantage point is up these steps. NOW COME ON! MOVE IT!"

There were four rooms on the second level. The master, a guest room, the study and a bathroom. Ross choose the masters where he and Junior moved two large dressers to barricade the door. The old man was placed in a huge walk-in closet that use to be his wife's. "You'll be safer in here, Mr. Crain," Ross assured before closing the door.

218

Junior was crouching down by the window peeking out. "Who are those people?" he asked while observing what appeared to be shadows advancing inside the house.

"Is there any guns in the house?" Ross asked while checking his weapon.

"No. Mother hated guns so father made it a point not to bring any into...."

"QUIET!" Ross cautioned. It was at that moment when they heard movement down stairs inside the house.

"We should...."

"Shhh!" Ross warned again while cocking his semi-automatic nine millimeter. His clip only held twelve rounds. Five of which he already used. Leaving him with seven shots and one in the chamber. He had an extra clip, but left it in his over coat down-stairs in the closet.

When they heard foot-steps quietly advancing. Both men quickly moved over to the side of the door and nervously waited.

Junior looked around for someplace to hide, but the only other place besides the closet was under the bed. "Maybe we should ask them what they want?" he suggested.

"It's obvious what they want."

"What do they want?" Junior asked, but before he could get an answer? Bullets began forcing their way through the bedroom door. Junior cried, "OH MY GOD!" backing away from the door.

"GET DOWN!" Ross shouted. By the time Junior could react, several bullet caught him in the chest, face and neck. He was dead before hitting the floor. "GOT-DAMN-IT!" Ross cursed before diving behind the bed. After turning it over on its side for cover, He proceeded to return fire, "POP-POP! Com'on, you motherfuckers!" he shouted, letting off another round, "POP! We can do this until the police arrive! You ever hear of a little thing called cell-phones! POP-POP-POP!" Once the door finally fail off of its hinges. Ross jumped from behind the bed and open fire, "POP! POP! Click, Click," until he was out of bullets. The dressers they used to barricade the door had been slit in half by the heavy caliber bullets.

The house was completely dark and so quiet now, Ross could literally hear his heart beating as he stood in the middle of the room totally exposed. Just as he was about to take cover, a tall shadow entered the room. Ross slowly took a few steps back. Then came the roaring blast of a double barrow shotgun, "POW!" He saw the muzzle flashes long before the force of the impact lifted him off his feet and sent him flying out the second story bedroom window, backwards.

After the shooting finally stopped. The old man held his breath as footsteps quietly moved throughout the room. He silently prayed for the assailants to leave the house, but knew that would be asking too much. Suspecting the assassins were there for his son, he knew it had everything to do with the lost shipment of drugs. Which was why he had Napo' call in a favor to retrieve it. Apparently it had been too late. His only son was dead. Murdered by the very people he choose to get in bed with. He cursed Junior for involving the family in his  shady deals.

He had never been a religious man, never had a reason to be. Now that it was just a matter of time before they found him hiding in the darkness of his bedroom closet. He thought a prayer might be appropriate.

After several minutes past. The old man thought his prayers had been answered. Just when he thought they had over looked the closet, the door slowly opened. He heard a voice say, "You can come out now." It was a female's voice.

Slowly, he crawled on his hands and knees until he was completely out of the closet. "I don't have a weapon. I am unarmed!" He shouted with nervousness in his frail voice. Except for a flash-light shining in his face, the room was pitch dark. He could tell there was someone standing in front of him. He shields his eyes from the bright light, but still couldn't make out the face. "Patti?" he uttered. "Is that you?"

# CHAPTER 15

Asmar waited ten more minutes before checking to see if Vicki was ready. As he sat there in his newly acquired ride. The weed from the spliff he had been toking on was beginning to make him paranoid. He thought about the conversation he just had with E-Man and wondered if he had done the right thing. E-Man seemed pretty upset after he told him who was actually responsible for the murder of his brother. Asmar begged him not to do something stupid, especially at the hotel.

"Yo, E," he remembered saying. "You can't push her at the hotel. Not unless you wanna' get caught? My people just paid me to drop her off at the airport. If I don't? They gonna' know something ain't right and start looking at me, yo? Chill, my dude! She's coming back. When she do, I'll let you know. Cool?"

"Young'en, you done lost your damn mind!" E-Man spat back. "I just paid you five grand for information I waited over a year to get. You think umma' risk blowing my chance to end the mutha' who murked my brutha'?"

Asmar remembered how angry E-Man was when he got out of the car and headed in the direction of Vicki's hotel. He took one more toke off the spliff before exiting his car. "Damn, I hope that ass-hole ain't do something stupid?" he mumbled on his way to the hotel while wishing he had waited before giving E-Man the information.

As soon as he turned the corner onto Church Street. He smiled as soon as he saw Vicki waiting with her bags out front. There were no words to express how relieved he was to see E-Man had decided to listen to reason and wait until Vicki returned from her trip.

"You look like you're surprised to see me," she studied his expression.

Unsure what she meant, he nervously asked, "Surprise? Why... why you say that?"

"I don't know. You just seemed surprised when you saw me, that's all."

He smiled uneasily. "Must be the new look," he said while grabbing her bags. As they casually walked around the corner to his car, he tried to make small talk. "Why the fuck are you sweating?"

"Probably from lugging my things by myself. I thought you said you were coming up to help me, or did you forget? You look like you been smoking that shit?"

He smiled. "My bad," he replied before changing the subject. "I don't know if I got the chance to tell you or not, but I was sorry to hear about, 'Face. I didn't know him like that, but Joey told me he was 'that dude'," he lied while opening the door on the passenger side. Even before Vicki got in, she could smell the weed he had been previously smoking. "I mean that in a good way," he continued before slamming the door shut behind her. Vicki watched him through the rear-view as he placed her bags in the trunk before getting into the car.

As they headed up Grand Street towards the highway. Asmar glanced at her as if he wanted to ask her something, but wasn't sure how to ask. Vicki, however, did not notice. She had been too preoccupied thinking about the man who just tried to murder her.

It happened just before leaving the suite. The moment she opened the door to leave, he was standing right there, waiting. "You looking for Camille?" she had asked him. Instead of an answer, he forced his way inside the suite and closed the door behind him. "Wait a minute! What the hell you doing?" she tried to stop him, but he had caught her completely off guard. "Are you crazy?" she asked. Instead of answering her he reached into his pocket and pulled out a pair of black leather gloves and took his time slipping them on. Vicki thought he looked familiar, but couldn't remember where she had seen him? "What do you want?" she asked. Still slipping on his gloves, he silently stared at her with such hatred, she knew only one of them would leave the suite alive. "Look, if it's money you want...." she tried to reason with him.

"Can you give me back my brutha's life?" he finally spoke. "If you can't. I'll take yours instead." He stepped up and shot a left jab to Vicki's face. He was fast with his hands, but Vicki swiftly moved to his right side and kicked him in the ribs with her left foot. "Ah!" he cried out in pain when two of his ribs cracked. Realizing his skills as a former street boxer was no match for the tall, beautiful woman who moved like an extreme boxer. He pulled out a huge knife and lunged at her. Vicki backed away while slipping out of her leather jacket. Rapping it around her left arm, she went completely into defense mode.

"You don't have to do this, you know. Just leave before..."

"Before what!" he snapped. "I slice you open?" He lunged at her again. Only this time, it was as if she had already anticipated all his moves. Stepping to the side, she grabbed the arm he held the knife in with one hand, while elbowing him in his face with her other. The knife flew out of his hand and he went down. Still holding on to his arm, she twist it in the opposite direction with very little effort until she heard a loud snap. "Ahhh!" he screamed. "Bitch! You broke my...." before he had a chance to finish what he was saying. She struck him in the throat, crushing his trachea. As his eyes widen with shock, he grabbed his throat in a desperate attempt to take air into his lungs while Vicki stood watching.

Once she was sure he was dead, she dragged his body out into the hall and propped it up next to the elevator for someone to eventually find.

She couldn't prove it, but something kept telling her Asmar had something, if not everything to do with the man who just tried to murder her. Mainly because, aside from the front desk, Camille, Cat' and her old-school crew, Asmar was the only other person who knew what room she was staying in.

"I still can't get over the new look," he finally worked up the nerve to say. What made you do it? You trying to catch?" he asked, trying to make small talk. When Vicki didn't answer, he pursued his last question. "You seeing somebody?"

Vicki glanced at him briefly, but said nothing.

"Oh, it's like that?"

"Like what?" she asked with annoyance.

"You know? The silent treatment. What? You upset with me, or something? 'Cause I damn sure don't remember crossing you. Actually, I've always been big on you. The only reason I never made my feelings for you known was because you were already taken. I respect O.B.P. You feel me?"

She looked at him and asked, "And what's O.B.P?"

"Other Brutha's Pussy," he laughed.

"Oh, so now I'm someone's pussy?" she asked, but regretted it afterwards.

"At the time, you were." He glanced at her and smiled. "I just mean... your heart belonged to 'Face and his to you."

She cut an eye at him. That was a nice sentiment, she thought. Something she would have never guessed he had in him. But just when she thought she had him figured out, he did, or said something that made her doubt her instincts.

"So what you think?" He asked.

She turned and looked at him. "About what?"

"Me feeling you?"

"I think you'll get over it soon enough." She turned towards the window again.

"So what you saying? Smooth joker like me ain't gotta' shot? Wait. Don't answer that. I just wanted you to know how I felt. I realize it might be a lil' too soon after your lost, but like I said, um' really feeling you. And if you ever need me, I'll be here for you. Cool?"

She wanted to say, "Whatever", but changed the subject instead. "You know a guy they call, Ghost?"

"Old-head?"

"Yeah."

"I know who you talking about. Why?"

"What about Bomani Africa, or his wife, Maria?"

Asmar smiled. "Big Keys? Yeah. What about 'em?"

"Big Keys?"

"Yeah. Baxter's big brutha'." He looked at her curious and asked, "You knew Baxter Keys?"

Vicki avoided making eye contact just in case. "I met him once. He tried to push up on me when I first arrived in town. Of course that was before I met 'Face," she lied.

Asmar smiled. "What made you choose 'Face over Baxter?"

"The caliber in the man."

Asmar smiled again. "I feel you. You did know them two jokers were boyz, right?"

"No, I didn't. And why you keep referring to Baxter in the past tense?"

He looked at her strangely and said, "Because he's history. I thought you knew?"

"Why would I?"

I don't know. Anyway, him and this joker he use to run with got into it. Papers said they killed each other," he laughed.

"You find that funny?"

"What's funny is how easily the pigs try to clear up a black on black. Picture two jokers killing each other. That kinda' thing don't even happen in the movies, you know?"

"So what do you think happened to them?"

"Baxter was my man, but he had a habit of running his mouth. If he thought it made him look good, he would tell your business, mine's and everybody else. Hell... he'll probably tell on himself if he thought it would boost his street rep. That's the kinda' guy he was. You do the math." Vicki glanced at him and rolled her eyes while thinking how much she couldn't stand him. "But his brother, Big Keys?" Asmar continued. "Is the SHIT! He legally changed his name in prison. I don't know his wife. I ain't even know the joker was married. Every time I see him, he either by his self, or got a bunch of ol' school killaz' rolling with him. The joker's a beast, yo. Type of guy you want on your team, know-I-mean?" He paused briefly before asking, "I don't mean to be nosy, or anything, but why you going to New Orleans? That's where you originally from?"

"Yeah," she said without going into any details.

As the car pulled up in front of the airort, Asmar asked, "You coming back, righ'?"

"I haven't decided yet." She quickly exit the car with her Carry-on and headed for the trunk to retrieve her luggage.

Asmar got out and helped her with her things. Before they parted. He whispered close to her ear, "I'll see you when you get back, Vicki. Don't forget what I said, okay?"

"Thanks for the ride, Mr. Bang," she said before disappearing through the entrance doors.

One half hour later, Asmar was back in Paterson taking his time cruising towards the east side. With a pocket full of money; the best weed money could buy, and a choice ride. He was feeling pretty good about himself.

As he cruised past Church street and saw several police cars and an ambulance parked in front of the Alexander hotel. His first thoughts were, a robbery gone bad, but that was neither here, nor there. He had no ententions of stopping until he saw Baby-Sams, Kenny Sams little brother standing around.

"What happened, yo'?" he asked the youth who seemed to have matured considerably since the last time Asmar saw him. Not only was the youth a little taller and had his weight up. Baby-Sams was dressed conservatively in a black full length single breasted coat that appeared to be cashmere. An expensive looking white cotton sweater. Dark-gray dress pant, and a pair of black high-end shoes.

"Don't know, son. Just got here myself, but somebody said one of the guest found a dead man in the hall on the fourth floor. I didn't see the body, but I heard it was a black man."

"Somebody must have O.D'ed in one of the rooms. Jokers ain't shit, yo. They could have just called 911 and left the fool in the room. Instead, they just kick his ass out in the hallway and left him for dead."

"I heard he was beaten to death."

"Beaten to death?" Asmar was confused now.

"That's what I heard, but you know how stories get twisted around. Know-I-mean?"

"I hear you. What you think really happened? A robbery gone bad? Asmar added before waiting to hear Baby-Sams take on the situation. "That type of shit bring mad heat, yo."

"Can't say. Must of been a walk-in, 'cause ain't nobody from the hotel know, or seem him before?"

"Is that right?" Asmar said while thinking. For a nanosecond, he found himself entertaining the possibility that Vicki took E-Man out. Until he remembered Baby-Sams telling him the victim was beaten to death. Even he had to laugh at such a ridiculous theory. After all, E-Man was a P-town living legend most men would have a problem pushing with a weapon.

They're probably in there right now trying to find out if anyone saw, or heard anything, know-I-mean?"

Asmar looked at him and said, "For somebody who just got here, you sure know a lot?"

Baby-Sams smiled and changed the subject. "Yo, who was that honey I saw you with about an hour ago?"

"An hour ago? How long you been around here? About an hour ago I took a friend to the airport from here. You saw us?"

"I was on my way downtown and saw you and this fine ass honey who looks just like this female who use to mess with my brutha', Kenny?"

Asmar looked at him strangely and asked, "How's he doing?"

"He's dead," said Baby-Sams.

"Dead! I thought you said he came out of the comma?"

"He did. After he got out of the hospital, he decided to get out of the game. A few weeks later, they found him dead in the streets. Somebody shot him in the head."

"Why the fuck I ain't hear nothing about it? I might have wanted to go to the funeral, you feel me?"

"N'all, son. It happen down the shore. In South Jersey. My people had his body moved down south and buried him next to my grandmother."

"Damn, lil bruh'. I'm sorry to hear that. So how you holding up? You a'ight?"

"I'm good, son."

Asmar looked up and saw the police looking their way. "I'm on my way up the hill. You need a ride?" he asked while turning to leave. He never noticed the young female who suddenly appeared and stood next to Baby-Sams'.

"We can use one. Good looking."

"We?" Asmar turned around and saw the attractive young beauty standing beside Baby-Sams.  Oh, shit!" he said with recollection. Where you come from?" he flirtatiously asked.

The young female gazed at Asmar with equal recollection but did not say anything.

"This my peoples, Bow," Baby-Sams introduced her.

Trapped into the bowlegged  beauty's gaze, Asmar was taken by complete surprise. "Nice to meet you, shorty. I'm Asmar," he said while wondering if she had remembered him.

"I know who you are," she said, blushing a little.

"As the three of them walked off down the street to the car. Asmar looked at her again and caught her sneaking peeks at him. He smiled to himself, then glanced at Baby-Sams, who seemed to be oblivious to the obvious chemistry between the two.

As they drove, Baby-Sams and his female companion sat up front. With Bow sitting between the two men, Asmar tried to engage her into conversation by asking, "Ain't you Debra Mathew lil' sista'?" When he notice her warm smile going cold. He knew he had phrased the question wrong.

"Why would you ask a question when you already knew the answer?" she rolled her eyes in anger.

Feeling as though he had played himself, Asmar glanced at Baby-Sams and could not stop wondering how a lame like Baby-Sams manage to bag a ghetto-star like Ms. Bow Mathews? "How far up y'all going?" he asked for a lack of anything else To say.

"Alabama projects?"

"You got that, Lil' Bruh." he replied, stealing a peek at the young Bow Mathews. He could tell she was still annoyed with him for referring to her as someone's lil' sista. He could also tell she was feeling him as much as he was feeling her. He thought about Punchie and her words of wisdom concerning Ms. Bow Mathew. That bitch might be fine, but trust me, son. You don't wanna' fuck with that. Ol' girl got issues, yo'.

As Bow sat quietly staring straight ahead. She waited until she was sure Baby-Sams was looking out the side window before stealing a peek at Asmar. She knew he liked her. She liked him, too, but feared he might think she was too young? She glanced down at his crotch with hopes of seeing a print, an out-line, anything that would give her some kind of inkling what Asmar was actually working with. But because of that ridiculous red, leather sweat-suit that was clearly two sizes too big for him, she was unable to tell. It didn't matter, though. She knew he was holding. He fooled around with too many high-caliber bitches who took good care of him not to be?

Baby-Sams found himself lost with thoughts of the woman he had seen Asmar with earlier. Since meeting her right after his brother, Kenny was released from the hospital. She was literally all he could think of. He knew the only way a guy like him would ever possess a woman like her? He had to step up his game tenfold and become his brother, Kenny on steroids. "You never told me who your friend was?" Baby-Sams couldn't resist asking.

"My friend?" Asmar was confused.

"Yeah. The one I saw you with earlier?"

"Oh, yeah. You talking about, Vicki Lane." He glanced at Bow and began volunteering information. "I did a favor for a friend of mine." The last thing he wanted, was for Bow to think he was not available. He then looked at Baby-Sams and asked, "You knew Londell Dixson? They called him, 'Face?"

"I know who you talking about," Baby-Sams replied. "You said her name was, Vicki?"

"Yeah. She was married to 'Face. They say she was with him when he got killed. If I'm not mistaken, I think she got a sister. Maybe Kenny use to go with her sister?"

"Maybe. The girl I'm talking  about name is Nemesis. She got real pretty eyes."

Asmar looked at him and asked, "Nemesis?"

"Yeah. Why? That's her sister?"

"Nemesis is Vicki," Asmar said. "She's the girl you saw me take to the airport. What make you think she was messing with your brutha?"

"That's what she told me?"

"When?"

"The same day you came through the Alabama and asked me how Kenny was doing. Remember? I told you he couldn't remember anything?"

"Yeah, yeah, I remember," Asmar lied.

"She came through a minute after you. Said she knew Kenny from back in the day. Said she heard he had gotten hurt and was wondering how he was doing."

"That was before Kenny got out of the hospital, right?"

"Yeah," Baby-Sams lied. "But I told her where she could find him once he got out."

"Why?"

"She asked. Said she stayed in Lakewood and wanted to know how far south Kenny was going in case she decided to look him up."

"She lied to you, lil' bruh'."

"Why you say that?"

"Because she ain't from Lakewood. Shit, she ain't even from Jersey, and she damn sure didn't know your brother."

"Why would she lie?"

"Hell if I know. That's something you gonna' have to ask her," Asmar said while parking near the Alabama projects.

As Baby-Sams quickly got out of the car. He thought about asking more questions about Nemesis, but decided against it. "It don't matter," said Baby-Sams while helping Bow out of the car.

Before pulling off, Asmar stole one last glance at Bow, then looked at Baby-Sams and said jokingly, "It does if she was the one who pushed him," then pulled off.

Baby-Sams was not laughing. He began to wonder what would make Asmar say something like that? Unless of course he knew something he wasn't telling?"

"What was that all about?" asked Bow.

Baby-Sams took Bow by the hand and said, "I think that ass-hole had something to do with Kenny's murder?"

"Why you say that?" asked Bow.

He thought about the last conversation he had with Asmar and began to get suspicious " Because the night Kenny was murked, Asmar had asked me a lot of questions earlier that day? Questions that had nothing to do with Kenny's well being. And that girl we were talking about? He said her name was Vicki. She told me her name was, Nemesis. She came through the 'Pound' minutes right after he left and start asking questions about Kenny. I'm beginning to believe it was him who sent that girl to get some information out of me about Kenny. And now he trying to deflect suspicion on to the girl probably because he know I'm on to his dirty-ass."

"You want me to stalk him tonight, Cuz'? I bet I can get the truth out of him for you."

Baby-Sams thought about it and realized Bow didn't have a bad idea. "I doubt if he'll admit to anything, but you can try," he replied as the two of them headed towards the Alabama project.

☥

Several hours later. Asmar sat in a pool-hall conversing with some buddies. When all of a sudden, he overheard some very unsettling news. E-Man had been found  dead at the Alexander Hotel this evening. No one actually knows how he had died. Some say he was shot, others had heard he'd gotten stabbed to death during a dispute.

"What you think happened, Az'?" asked one of the men Asmar had been talking with. Asmar's mind had drifted off to some-place else and never heard the question. "YO, AZ'!" the man shouted to get Asmar's attention.

"WHAT, FOOL! WHAT!" Asmar irritably shouted back.

"Damn, yo'. I asked what you thought happen to E'? You drifted off someplace else on us."

"Fuck if I know what happened to that dumb-ass-idiot." He then stood and immediately changed the subject, "I gotta' pick this chick' up and I'm ten minutes late. I'll get with you jokers later."

On his way to his car. He thought about Vicki's reaction upon his return to help her with her things. "No wonder she was suspicious of me," he muttered as he remembered. "She knows," he whispered under his breath.

As he drove around town weighing the prospects of Vicki coming after him. He knew he had to do something, and fast before she returned. Because if what they say about her had any truth to it. He was surely in trouble. The problem was, he just didn't know what to do. His thoughts were all over the place and leaving town was not an option.

He needed to take a step back and relax. He thought about smoking a 'blunt' but was afraid it would only make him more paranoid. He needed something to calm his nerves, fast.

He pulled over at the first liquor store he spotted. Just as he was about to get out of the car, he suddenly thought of Punchie's home-boy, Wreak and smiled.

Parked in the lot of the low income housing projects. The C.C.P. was the one place Asmar new to look for the youth. At the very least, he was hoping someone would tell him where Wreak could be found.

As he sat in his car listening to music while toking on a blunt and sipping cheap wine. He saw someone he couldn't resist hollering at. It was a female he had been trying to bag for some time now. But like all choice females chasing stacks. She was playing hard-to-get. Normally he would have said, "Fuck that bitch!" but the weed and wine that had his head in a twine convinced him otherwise.

Leading with his manhood. Asmar found himself rushing out of the car in pursuit of her when all of a sudden, a tall dark-skinned man with long, thick, rugged dreadlocks approached him.

"You Azmor?" the man asked with a heavy West Indies accent. At first Asmar didn't have a clue who the man was until he spoke again. "Young soldier 'ere tells me ya' might 'ave some information on my people's murdah'?" He directed Asmar's attention towards a black Benz' where Wreak was standing between two hard-looking Jamaicans foot-soldiers. The fear in Wreak's eyes told Asmar all he needed to know about the three men.

"Fuck you mean, information! What I look like? Some type of informant! You jokers got the game twisted! You must be cops!" Asmar played the 'hard card' just to see what he was working with.

"Wha'cha talkin' 'bout cops, Bee!" he looked at Wreak and said, "Me thought yah' said your man was official, Wreak? Me come in peace and he go and insult us."

"No disrespect yo'," Asmar spoke up quickly before it got out of hand. "I just don't know you fools."

"Before yah' open your mouth with that slick Yankee talk yah' talkin'. One ting' yah' gotta' know 'bout Khaleff. Me ain't nobody's fool. Me straight shotta, yah' 'ear me. Come to bust this Yankee shit-'ole wide open, seen'?" He cut an eye at Wreak and said, "Me starting to detect a little 'ostility from your boy, Wreak?"

Before Wreak could reply, Asmar quickly restated. "Again, yo. No disrespect. I just ain't use to jokers rolling up on me in the street."

"Would yah' rather we rolled up on yah' at yah' 'ouse?"

"Hell no! But I see your point. Tell you what. Why don't we take a ride in my car. Wreak and your people can follow in yours."

Khaleff studied Asmar while giving his proposal deliberate and careful thought. Not because he was apprehensive about taking a ride with Asmar without his men. He just wasn't sure if Asmar was wasting his time.

"He's official, Khaleff," yelled Wreak from the side-line.

Without taking his eyes off of Asmar, the man who went by the name, Khaleff replied, "'For your sake, 'e betta' be."

Asmar drove Khaleff around town spinning a tale about a ruthless female killer  who went by the name of, Nemesis. It was his way of dealing with Vicki before she returned from her trip and dealt with him for putting E-Man on her.

Khaleff thought about it and now had the name of the woman who hung up on him right after pushing Spivey Wise. "Who she be workin' for?" he immediately asked.

"That information I don't have, but if I had to take a guess, his name would be SunRise." Asmar smiled at how well everything was coming together for him. He didn't have a beef with SunRise personally. It was just business and the only rational explanation that would be credible enough for Khaleff to believe.

"Who is this SunRise and why him put a price on me people's head?"

"Like I said. I don't know who put the tag on your boy's head. I do know she put in some work for SunRise before. Which was why I said, if I had to guess, and I stress the word, guess. His name would be, SunRise.

"Who is this blood-clot?"

 "Some young, rich, joker' who hates the drug game."

And this SunRise was also responsible for paying the woman to push Spivey's rival, Michael 'Enderson?"

242

"I'd be lying if I said I knew the answer to that question. Shit, I'm guessing he was the one who hired Nemesis to push your people? Again, I emphasize the word, guessing."

"So... you can't be sure?"

"I was told you were seeking information concerning the death of Spivey Wise, and willing to pay ten grand for it. I already told you who, how and why your man was pushed."

"Me believe you. Where can I find this woman and 'er employer?"

"I was told she just left town. When she'll be back, is anyone's guess? But SunRise is around. If I'm not mistaken, he has an apartment in building four of the C.C.P."

At first, Khaleff had believed everything Asmar had told him. But when Asmar said she just upped and left town? He suddenly had his doubts. "Drive up the street and pull over."

Asmar drove a few blocks up the street and pulled over to the curb. Khaleff got out of the car and produced half of the money he promised. "That's 'alf. You get the other 'alf after we find 'er, If me can't find 'er. Me 'ave no problem finding you, seen'?" He then slammed the door shut and walked off to his awaiting car.

## *To be continued....*

# NEMESIS III

To order copies of Tehuti Atum-Ra's first book, please send check or money order to:

**Midnight Express Books**
**POBox 69**
**Berryville AR 72616**

Nemesis          Nemesis II The FOLD

QTY ORDERED

| | | | |
|---|---|---|---|
| _____ | NEMESIS | $14.95 | $_____ |
| _____ | NEMESIS II The FOLD | $14.95 | $_____ |
| | | Subtotal | $_____ |

How many books are you ordering          _____ x $3.99 =     $_____
MEB order processing fee          _____ x $1.50 =     $_____

TOTAL ENCLOSED $_____

Ship to:
NAME _____

ADDRESS _____

_____

# NEMESIS III

www.ingramcontent.com/pod-product-compliance
Lightning Source LLC
Chambersburg PA
CBHW060308260626
47160CB00007B/2543